Son of Defiance
Emil Schellhase

A CIVIL WAR NOVEL

Mae Durden-Nelson

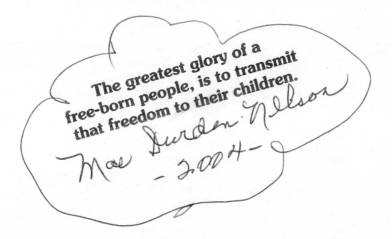

The greatest glory of a free-born people, is to transmit that freedom to their children.

Mae Durden-Nelson

— 2004 —

NORTEX PRESS ★ NORTEX Austin, Texas

This book is a work of fiction set in the times, places, events, and situations as historically accurate as was possible. Names of the characters, while they were actual names of persons living at that time and place, are purely fictional. The names have been used to lend authenticity to the story and to commemorate and celebrate the positive implications of their heroic past. Any resemblance to actual persons, living or dead, is purely coincidental.

Cover photo: Dakota Durden of Comfort, Texas, and grandson of author. He is posing as Emil Schellhase, the main character in this fictitious story, *Son of Defiance*. Dakota is holding an authentic Civil War muzzle-loading powder rifle, which belongs to his family. *Photo by Bill Nelson.*

FIRST EDITION
Copyright © 2004
By Mae Durden-Nelson
Manufactured in the U.S.A.
By Nortex Press
A Division of Sunbelt Media, Inc.
Austin, Texas
ALL RIGHTS RESERVED.
1-57168-837-4
Library of Congress Control Number: 2004104000

ALSO BY MAE DURDEN-NELSON
I Just Called Her Momma

Dedication

Treue der Union
(True to the Union)

The Treue der Union Monument in Comfort, Texas—dedicated August 10, 1866—stands as a symbol to one of the most dramatic events in the Hill Country's history. The monument is dedicated to those men from Comfort, Sisterdale, Fredericksburg, and the surrounding area who were sympathetic to the Union cause during the Civil War and who died for their beliefs in The Battle of the Nueces, August 10, 1862.

Along with such places as Gettysburg and Pearl Harbor, the United States Flag flies at half-staff in perpetuity at the monument site.

—From Comfort Chamber of Commerce brochure

This book, while fiction, considered the women and children who were left behind to care for each other while the above events in history were taking place.

This book is dedicated to all the women and children who were left behind then, and to all those who must stay behind today and care for their families when a war for freedom is fought.

Acknowledgments

My grateful thanks, first of all, to George Hale. When I forgot to save the first draft of this novel in my computer, George magically resurrected my original manuscript from that mysterious hungry monster known as cyberspace! Here's to you, George. Without your tedious work, I would never have completed this novel.

Also, special thanks to my architect husband, Bill Nelson, for his encouragement, advice, and suggestions for the plot problems of this novel. He gave inspiration for the "hollowed-out stone" and the "milk paint" ideas. His architectural concept of the possible remains of a burned 1850s pioneer home was most helpful.

My heartfelt gratitude to Laura Rhodes, for giving me generous access to her translation of the original copy of *1846 Fritz Schellhase Diary*, an amazing document which begins in Brandenburg, Germany, and follows an immigrant to Comfort, Texas.

Special thanks also to Paul Burrier for the use of

his vast research papers and who gave inspiration to create this story in the first place.

Also, a great big thank you goes to Claire Vaughan of San Antonio, Texas, for sending me the excerpt of the *Autobiography of Ed Steves* of Comfort. Ed Steves was her husband's great-great-grandfather. It contained valuable information that helped shape my story.

After the writing of the story had ended and as the final pages were being prepared for the printer, two dear and wonderful friends from Comfort, Texas, namely Elizabeth Seidensticker and her daughter Carolyn Spenrath, came to show me a wonderful wedding picture of her relative—the *real Emil Schellhase and his bride*! Thank you, Elizabeth and Carolyn!

I also gratefully acknowledge my indebtedness to my critique group members in San Antonio, Texas: Art Grand, Joyce Williams, Dr. Maritha Burmeister, and Priscilla Kohutek. Your valuable critiques made this work a joy and, hopefully, improved its readability. Thanks, guys.

Finally, my deepest indebtedness to Gregory J. Krauter of Comfort for his final critique of my completed manuscript. His notations helped me add to the circle of historic events in the plot of this novel. His willingness to write the foreword makes the adventure of this book memorable for me.

Foreword

It is a regrettable fact that, along with love and many other good as well as bad traits of human nature, war has been present since before the beginning of recorded history. One could also maintain that advances in technology have primarily defined the overwhelming majority of related changes over the ages, and especially during the last century. Furthermore, certain wars and significant conflicts have always been deemed to be unusually unique or memorable.

One excellent example is the American Civil War (War Between the States), which in overall context took place in relatively recent history and close geographic proximity. With the greatest number of large or decisive battles and actions having mostly taken place in relatively established states located east of the Mississippi River, there has been a great lack of attention given to events and persons in the westerly frontier states and territories. This is especially prevalent with respect to the beautiful Hill Country region in Central Texas.

Peaceful immigrants of predominately German descent—between the latter 1840s and the outbreak of the Civil War—originally settled this particular area. Many were well educated and skilled individuals whose lives and futures, in varying degrees, had been or would be greatly influenced by the failed German revolution of 1848. After enduring generations of poverty, famine, overcrowded conditions, and, above all, an almost total lack of individual freedoms in Europe, all had grown desperate for a better quality of life with greater opportunities for themselves, their families, and their descendants. Every one of these immigrants risked not only their own lives but also often their entire families', during the long and dangerous voyages by sea to this new environment. Many of the immigrants, especially those who had not been part of any organized settlement plan, would eventually help to colonize a severe and unknown frontier wilderness. Within the span of about a decade, a number of these idealistic and innovative new immigrants were able to achieve an almost utopian lifestyle—until the confusion and uncertainties of Civil War began to appear on the horizon and within time grew to permanently influence and forever change the area.

Mae Durden-Nelson has utilized her creative abilities to compose a stimulating Civil War–era saga that contains fictional characters and the complete spectrum of human emotions in exciting and historically accurate settings and backgrounds. This book, while focusing primarily upon youthful characters, should enjoy wide appeal among all age groups, at the same time serving to better educate the public about one of the most horrendous events endured by any of the areas of settlement along the frontier wilderness during the Civil War.

Mae Durden-Nelson has also infused her work with a multitude of details unique to the German spirit. Her special knowledge and insight relative to the remarkable history of the community of Comfort and surrounding areas in Central Texas is quite evident. She has included many time-honored traditions and customs which can only be learned and fully appreciated though a lifetime of exposure to such a cultural environment combined with a special awareness of its true value. This book will contribute considerably to a rather limited but gradually increasing body of literature relating to a particular area, and its people and history, which has not previously received the attention that it is most certainly due.

It has been my pleasure to read this distinctive book, and I am honored to have the opportunity to make but a small contribution to this important accomplishment.

GREGORY J. KRAUTER
Comfort, Texas
October 4, 2003

Chapter One
Comfort, Texas
1862

It was past midnight, but sleep would not come. Emil flipped to his left side and punched his fist into the goose down pillow, the one luxury he'd been allowed to bring from Germany. *I should just run away.* He punched the pillow again. *But where to? I have to stay in Texas. I have no choice. But someday, when I am older and braver, I will return to my homeland.*

Nothing of this was right—or necessary. However, no matter how Emil pleaded, Papa had saddled his horse that morning and rode away.

"Emil," he had said, "it will be up to you to take care of this farm and our family for a while. I have no choice. I have a duty, and I must go. Our freedom is being threatened. Obey your mother, son. Do your best, that's all I ask of you."

But Papa did have a choice! He didn't have to take sides. That business about keeping slaves didn't need to concern him—not here in the beautiful countryside just outside of Comfort, Texas. The Schellhase farm was considered the most prosperous one in the community—and they built it without benefit of slaves. Hard work and good old German fortitude created it. So why didn't Papa mind his own business about others owning slaves? Only a few families in Comfort owned them.

Emil remembered how he met up with one of those black boys one day down at the Cypress Creek. They were both fishing—on opposite sides of the creek. He waved a greeting at the boy. When the boy did not wave back, Emil decided the black boy was simply shy. There were shallow stepping stones just below the place where they were fishing, Emil waded across to make acquaintance with him. When the boy saw Emil coming, he grabbed up his fishing pole and ran off into the underbrush along the creek. Emil shouted at him to wait: "I just want to talk."

But the boy was gone, and Emil was not allowed to wander off into the woods. In truth, he was forbidden to even cross the creek. Emil returned to his side of the meandering stream and continued fishing. He had dismissed that event . . . until tonight . . . beyond midnight . . . unable to sleep . . . old memories swarmed his mind.

Why, Papa, why? Why did you leave? Tears welled up in Emil's eyes.

And that other business—about Texas wanting to secede from the United States. So what? All Texans were ordered to take a loyalty oath to the newly formed Confederacy. So what? What did it matter? A lot of men took that oath only to keep their homes and families from harm. After that, they were free to stay home with their families where they belonged!

But not Papa! Papa raged on and on. "We must rebel against these tyrants! They're traitors to our new freedom." He expounded on the subject anywhere he could get an audience.

Nein! Nein! Nein! *This time, Papa, you are wrong. A good father does not leave. It would have been better to give in—do nothing to antagonize—*

A sudden noise outside made Emil jump from his bed. Something was upsetting the horses inside the barn. They were secured—he had taken care of that himself. There were, after all, still occasional thefts by roaming renegade bands of Indians.

Emil stepped to the small loft window. Though the moonlight, he squinted to see the barn. He could hear nothing more. There was a faint glow on the northern horizon, but he was too distraught to worry about that. He shrugged his shoulders and slouched back to bed.

Was he imagining things? He took a deep breath. He hated this wretched feeling inside. Was it never going to let him sleep?

Emil had just crawled back into bed when he heard it again. This time there was no doubt. Some horses were out of the barn and were being ridden away! He heard the saddles creaking! That sound was unmistakable.

Emil grabbed his trousers. While pulling them on, he scrambled down from the loft. His momma was standing at the window holding the rifle.

"Emil! The horses—"

"*Ja, ja.* Give me the gun, Momma."

"No, Emil. It might be Indians."

"But the horses—Momma! We can't lose them."

"And I can't lose you! Let them have the horses. Just pray they'll leave us our barn—our house. Take the rifle, Emil, but you stay here with Meta and me. We'll watch together. If they come back, we'll shoot."

Emil and his mother sat side by side, watching and waiting in terrible silence. Little Meta never stirred in the pretty little cypress wood bed Papa had built for her.

Chapter Two

Emil heard his mother cracking twigs to start a fire in the fireplace. He was awake instantly. The rifle was no longer in his arms.

"Momma? Where's the rifle? I must go out to see about the—"

"I've been out. Two of our horses are gone, along with two saddles—"

"Saddles, too? Those redskins."

"No, Emil. Not Indians. I found this on a nail by the barn door."

She handed Emil the tattered piece of paper. On it was scribbled, "We need more horses. We will make it up to you when we return from the war. We are sorry for this. Be careful. Destroy this note. Uncle Edgar and Bruno."

Emil threw the paper on the rough-hewn table with a vengeance. "*Das ist verrückt!* (This is crazy.) *Das ist jeszt genug!* (That is enough now). Stealing from one's own family! Momma, I'm going to town to get help. We'll catch those thieves."

His mother grabbed his arm, "No. Emil! You must not be seen in Comfort today! You don't understand."

"You are right, Momma. I don't understand. I don't!" His voice cracked, and that embarrassed and angered him even more.

"Emil, not so loud. You'll wake your sister."

Emil dropped into the chair with the cowhide seat. Any other time his mother would have lectured him for such rude and disrespectful behavior. Instead, she rushed to his side to console him. He pushed her away with more force than he intended. His mother gasped in shock.

"Emil! What is wrong with you? Your Papa said—"

"I know what Papa said. He shouldn't have left us, Momma! It's not right."

Emil sobbed with sudden, violent tears. More ashamed than ever, he pushed back his chair and it crashed to the floor. He bolted out the door and stumbled toward the barn. His mother followed him to the door but stopped. *Let him cool down*, she thought. He was, after all, still a boy. He was too young for this much responsibility. And he was right. His father should not have left them.

Emil's tears blinded him as he opened the heavy barn door. The sweet, musty fragrance of new hay met his nostrils, but he was so incensed he could not enjoy his favorite aroma.

Two of the four horse stalls were indeed empty. But, he observed, the back double doors of the barn were not only closed but they were latched from the inside. *That's strange. Thieves steal your horses and then close the doors? No, Momma must have done that.* What difference did it make anyway? Two horses were gone.

Emil kicked a half-empty grain bucket and sent it flying across the barn floor; the oats left a trail. Some of it showered over Emil's blond hair, and the dust of the grain stuck to his cheeks, wet from falling tears. The bucket clacked and clanged as it scooted and hit the nearby wall.

"*Verdammte Texas!*" he shouted between sobs at the top of his voice.

In the milking stall, Bessie raised her head and answered him in a loud *s-u-u-k-k-k*. At any other time, he would have spoken to the gentle milk cow. Instead, Emil threw himself into a nearby pile of old hay and buried his face in his arms. He sobbed unchecked—as one without hope—until he felt a hand on his back.

"Leave me alone, Momma."

"I'm so sorry, Emil." Her words were soft and gentle, and he recognized her voice immediately. He sat up in a hurry and wiped his eyes with his sleeve.

"Elizabeth Boerner! What are you doing here?'

Elizabeth dropped to her knees beside him. "Oh, Emil," she sobbed. "They burned our house last night. Our house and barn, everything is gone. Papa—Papa was out feeding the oxen when—they rode up and—they tied him up—they took him away!"

Elizabeth spoke between gasps of breath. Her eyes were open wide. She was near hysteria. She dropped to the barn floor and held her head in dismay.

Emil felt a strange ripple go through his body. He didn't know how to comfort her. "Why didn't you come to our house—instead of this barn?"

"I was afraid, Emil. Papa often told me—if they ever came for him—I was to sneak out and run to your house. I was doing what he told me to do, but before I could get to your house, I saw two men opening your barn doors and taking your horses. I was so scared and confused! I hid in the shadows of the trees until they were gone. I guess I was too frightened to think clearly. Later, I slipped inside and crawled up there to the loft to hide."

"The men who stole our horses were Uncle Edgar and Bruno. Our own relatives!"

"Oh Emil. What is happening to all our grownups? It's crazy. People have lost their senses. Sometimes I think my momma was the lucky one. I'm so sad she died from cholera, but at least she won't know all this insane fighting. We were all good friends once—before we left Germany. Why can't they remember the promises they made to each other?"

Emil sat down beside her and picked up a piece of the hay.

"I don't know, Elizabeth. My papa is gone, too. He left yesterday."

Her voice softened. "I know. Papa told me he was going. Oh, Emil. Do you remember? We made a vow too—you and I." Elizabeth smiled even though her eyes were still glistening wet with tears.

Emil saw her sad smile and felt his face grow warm. *Schwindelkopf (dizzy-headed)*, he thought. He knew he was blushing but couldn't stop. Lizzy always did that to him! Those pale blue eyes!

He squirmed and pulled his long legs under his chin. "We were just little children then, Lizzy. It was silly."

Elizabeth smoothed out her dress over her knees as she sat cross-legged beside him. "I'm sorry to hear you say that. It wasn't silly, Emil. At least I didn't think so."

"Well, never mind that now." Emil stood up, eager to change the topic. "We've got to find your father. Who took him; did you recognize them—or know them?"

"No, it was too dark, and I was too scared. They didn't talk German, though. I could hear that."

"Well, let's go to the house and tell Momma you're here. We should not speak about this in front of little Meta, though. Maybe you can say you were going for a walk and we just happened to meet. Come, Meta will be happy to see you."

Emil helped Elizabeth up. He was very conscious of her small hand in his. Yes, of course he remembered the vow they'd taken back on the ship. Her hand was in his then, too . . .

"*Mach schnell*, Emil." Elizabeth was up and walking toward the barn door before Emil could take a step. He always felt so clumsy next to her! Why was it, he wondered, that girls were so quick and light on their tiny feet? Hers were only half as large as his, and already she was at the door, waiting for him to open it.

Momma must have seen them coming as the door to the house opened wide and little Meta came running toward them. She skipped toward Lizzy, laughing and yelling, and her golden curls bounced. "Lizzy! Lizzy! Carry me piggyback, please."

Elizabeth scooped Meta up in her arms and the two girls hugged. Emil, ahead of the girls now, put his finger to his lips in signal to Momma not to ask questions. "I'll tell you later," he whispered quickly.

Chapter Three

Meanwhile, two miles away, the little hamlet of Comfort, Texas, was just beginning to come to life. Smoke was spiraling out of the rock chimneys of several neat fachwerk homes along the rutted main street. The morning sun had not yet shown itself, but several dogs were barking, for whatever reason dogs exercise their lungs at daybreak.

Joining the dogs' chorus, a rooster crowed at the Faltin house. It was answered by another crowing at the Wiedenfelds'. Then the milk cow in the Altgelts' barn raised its voice in a long *sch-uuk, sch-uuk* to tell her owner that it was milking time. Her calf, in another pen, chorused in with its plea for breakfast.

Along the banks of the Cypress Creek, which meandered not far from the tiny settlement, early-morning birds were chirping and flitting about. Ducks quacked and geese honked their good mornings to each other while sliding into the cool water of the creek. They alternated floating and ducking their heads underwater. Finally, not to be left out of the opus, horses in

11

their stalls could be heard whining to complete the animals' discordant symphony.

In one barn however, up on Main Street, behind the Brinkmanns' home, two horses did not whinny. They were standing still, with their heads in a rest pose. They had been ridden hard—not too long ago.

Meanwhile, inside the cellar, beneath the Brinkmanns' *fachwerk* cabin, several men spoke just above a whisper in nervous and excited voices.

"Has anyone heard from Herr Boerner? He should have been here hours ago." The young voice belonged to Bruno Degener.

Young Karl Vater answered in a low whisper, "I am afraid for him. He's been our faithful messenger and provider of advice and food for our journey."

"If his activities have been discovered . . ." Edgar Degener shook his head and stroked his reddish-black beard.

Emil's father, Fritz Schellhase, interrupted. "I agree, the man is brave to assist us. But people who know him realize he has his hands full with no wife and a young daughter to care for. Even *die Hängerbande*, in all their cruelty, surely would not bother him, or even suspect him of anything." Fritz Schellhase flashed a sudden smile. "Besides, he talks so little that—"

Degener said in a slow cadence, "That is true. But my friends, he should have been here by now."

Young Vater stood up. "If I may take a fresh horse, I'll ride out to check on him. It's not far to his farm."

"That's a good idea," Emil's father said with obvious authority. "But you must not ride out of town in haste. You act like nothing is different today. No one must suspect our plans. Meanwhile, we'll continue to pack what supplies we have assembled for the trip. We must be ready to ride by dark tonight."

Karl Vater saddled a fresh horse at once and rode down the peaceful, quiet main street of Comfort. Frau Faltin, out sweeping the sand in her front yard, waved and nodded at Karl. He tipped his hat and rode by slowly without stopping to visit. His mission was clear: Find Herr Boerner.

Chapter Four

Karl sat straight in the saddle, holding the reins in his right hand and resting his left hand on his thigh. He cut a dashing figure on horseback. He was a confident and handsome young bachelor who knew his own mind.

Karl's decision to desist from bearing arms against his newly adopted country of America was strong. His family had forever left behind in Germany the awful shackles of political, religious, social, and economic slavery. He would not now sit by and condone human slavery on American soil.

Some time ago, March 16, 1861, Karl, on business in Brenham, Texas, chanced upon an occasion to hear Governor Sam Houston speak. Because he, too, had refused to take the oath of allegiance to the new Confederate government, Houston had been ousted as governor of Texas. However, through a bit of politics, Houston was one of the few citizens granted the privilege of traveling about in Texas as a free citizen.

Sam Houston, having left Austin for his home near

Huntsville, had stopped for a day's rest in Brenham. Former comrades and old friends asked Houston to speak his sentiments. He refused until some hotheads declared he should not be allowed to speak. This aroused the ire of the old lion-hearted hero, and he was proud to agree to speak.

The excitement was intense. Groups gathered in the streets of Brenham and shouted that it would be treason against the Confederate government to permit Governor Houston to speak against secession.

Karl Vater was swept along with the crowds that soon packed the courthouse. As Houston rose to speak, cries were heard.

"Put him out!"

"Don't let him speak!"

"Kill him!"

At that moment Mr. Hugh McIntyre, a wealthy planter and leading secessionist, sprang up on a table and drew a large Colt revolver.

"I and a hundred other friends of Governor Houston invited him to address us, and we will kill the first man who insults or who may attempt to injure him. I, too, think Governor Houston ought to have accepted the situation and taken the oath of allegiance to our Confederate government, but he thought otherwise. He is an honest and sincere man, and he has shed his blood for Texas independence. There is no other man who has more right to be heard by the people of Texas. Now, fellow citizens, give him your close attention, and you ruffians, keep quiet or I myself will kill you!"

As Karl rode slowly along the banks of Cypress Creek on his way to find Herr Boerner, his heart raced as he remembered that incident and the speech. The crowd, pressed right up against the speaker's platform, had shoved him along. He could have reached out and touched Sam Houston's boots! To see that big man in such close proximity; to hear him expound in that great, powerful voice of his the same exact thoughts of his own heart—Karl's own convictions and ideals were reinforced and confirmed. From that day on, he had known what he must do: Join the Union forces!

As Karl rode from Comfort, he observed how clear the sky was that morning. The weather was cooperating for tonight's journey. He wondered briefly how many Union supporters would finally join them.

But first things first. He must decide his strategy to find Herr Boerner. The Boerner farm was located two miles north of Comfort, toward the North Creek community. Should he go directly there? Or should he take the less likely and longer approach from the west? If he continued alongside Cypress Creek—would it be possible he might come across a fresh trail made during the night?

Karl considered himself a good tracker. Nevertheless, finding Herr Boerner was a special challenge. Boerner's genius for bringing in supplies and food was known throughout the organization. He was known to take unusual approaches to the many places where compatriots were hiding out in the woods around

Comfort. So, Karl reasoned, Herr Boerner probably would not have taken the most logical or the shortest route into Comfort last night to bring them supplies.

He decided finally to save time and go directly to the Boerner farm. Elizabeth would be able to tell him not only what time Herr Boerner had departed yesterday evening, but also perhaps give a clue to which direction he might have taken. That decision made, Karl began to trot the horse a bit faster.

He had traveled about a mile when he became aware of smoke. The smell of something burned or burning made him stop the horse.

They stood perfectly still, and Karl raised his head and sniffed in several directions as he listened. Hearing nothing out of the ordinary, he proceeded at a slower pace. Yet a premonition of danger made him decide to go no farther on horseback. He would make less noise continuing on foot.

Karl tied his horse to a tree. His senses were keen and alert to every sound. The closer he came to the Boerner place, the stronger the smell of burned timber.

He soon came to the place where Herr Boerner had chopped down trees to put in a new field. Karl sucked in his breath. Across the clearing, the simple *fachwerk*-and-stone house was still smoldering. The fireplace and two walls still stood as mute testimony to what once was a frontier dwelling. Here and there, small flames still flickered and licked at the collapsed frame of a once-proud barn.

Karl stood frozen, hiding behind the trunk of a

large live-oak. Now what? Where was Herr Boerner? And where was Elizabeth? Was this the work of Indians? An accidental fire? God forbid, the *Hänger-bande*?

Karl stayed hidden for five or more minutes, standing perfectly still and watching for any sign of life or movement. After a while, he decided to use the shelter of the trees and underbrush to circle the area to inspect the scene more closely. The ominous feeling of danger was acute.

That's when he heard the snap of a twig—very close behind him.

Chapter Five

Emil's head was surprisingly clear after so little sleep the night before. He remembered that he must quickly milk the cow before he could speak further with his mother about Lizzy's father. He'd been able to cover only a few of the details while Lizzy kept Meta busy playing a game outdoors.

Emil milked the gentle cow—an act so automatic he hardly realized he was doing it. Meanwhile, his mind was frantic for ideas. What he could do to find Lizzy's father? If the *Hängerbande* had seized him, where would they be taking him?

Papa had discussed many of the existing contentions within the small community of immigrants, and Emil did know a few facts—according to his father, at least.

One thing was certain, there were many German neighbors who wanted no part in this bigger disagreement within the state of Texas—that of the secession of Texas from the Union. Emil wished now he had listened a bit more intently to the names of people sympathetic to the Union cause. At the time, he'd been more interested in fishing or swimming with the neighborhood boys.

Papa did indicate on a few occasions—especially when they were taking the wagon into Comfort to buy supplies, that there was one friendly person Emil could trust for help. Emil remembered how those trips always included a stop at Altgelt's Mill for a sack of cornmeal.

Emil's memory was vague about other things, too. It seemed to him the trips into Comfort had come more often recently and that the talk between the grownups had become more intense. It embarrassed Emil how worked-up his father became on a few occasions, how he seemed to almost forget that his son was riding beside him on the spring seat. He watched in alarm when his father drove the horses with a whip and angry commands. Sometimes Emil wished he'd stayed at home.

Emil remembered, too, that of late his mother often looked like she'd been crying. When Emil asked her what was wrong, she simply raised her head and looked at him with weary eyes and sighed, *"Ach, lassen sie mich in Ruhe!"* (Just leave me alone!)

He had also observed how lately his momma and papa would be in a deep discussion about something and when he came near enough to understand words, they'd stop and change the subject.

Well, if they thought I was not aware, they should think again. It only made me more curious about what was happening. But, being a German-bred youth, he kept his thoughts to himself and did not ask questions of his parents or elders. Parents were the ultimate decision-makers, and a respectful son or daughter did not question their authority.

One morning when Emil had been up in the loft of the barn catching mice, he kept his silence and did not give away his presence when his mother and father entered the barn, already arguing in short, clipped sentences.

"But if you go, what will happen with this farm?" His mother's bonnet did not allow Emil to see her face or her blazing red hair beneath it.

"Boerner will be here to take care of both our places. And Emil is well trained. Why, he's almost a man. He will manage. Our son can ride and shoot as well as any young man I know. Emil has a good head on his shoulders."

Emil smiled, very proud of himself. His father had never said that to his face.

"But what about little Meta? What about me? And Emil is not a young man as you say. He is only fourteen—he needs his father."

"It's because of all of you that I must go. There are forces in our new land that intend to make us out as traitors to our adopted country. We have not come to Texas to be made sport of. A German in America has his integrity to uphold, for our own welfare and our children's future."

"But some men are taking the so-called oath of

allegiance to that confounded Confederacy. That frees them from entering the argument over what is right and wrong. Why can't you do likewise?"

"A man has to do what a man has to do. I cannot speak out of both sides of my mouth. Emma, I will not discuss this anymore! The Union must be preserved. I am asking for your support—not arguments about what I must do or not do."

"I will give you my support. But inside, Fritz, I am against your leaving. Oh, now I wish we were back in Germany!"

"Leibe Frau, have you forgotten how bad it was there? We had nothing! *No hope!* Now, look around this place here! We have a comfortable home and beautiful children who have a school to attend in Comfort. And look at these wonderful hills and surroundings. Here you have peace, your flowers and a yard and your geese and—"

"But if you leave us—oh, Fritz—"

"I will come back, Emma. This conflict can't last long. You'll see. I will return."

"I can see it's useless to argue with you. Go, then. But if you get killed—I'll never—I'll never—speak to you again!"

With that pronouncement, Momma stomped her foot and ran from the barn. Emil couldn't see his father's face, but he could certainly imagine the firmness of his jaw and how steady and fierce his eyes blazed in determination. Yes, that was a familiar look. Not many dared to argue with Fritz Schellhase.

Stretched out on his stomach there on the loft floor that day, he had watched his father leave the barn. Emil then put his head down on his arms folded in front of himself. *I am not ready to be a man—I'm not ready to face such conflict.*

That night at the supper table, Papa gave Emil reminders and asked him questions about his working knowledge of the farm:

"How much do you feed the horses?"

"When do you feed the animals?"

"You must keep the milk cow away from her calf during the day or there'll be no milk."

"Gates must always be kept secured or livestock will get mixed up. When animals see an open gate, they run to escape."

"Help Momma with heavy lifting."

"If the meat supply runs low, you must kill a deer."

"You remember how to butcher a deer and skin it?"

Emil's voice broke several times under the pressure of his father's quiz, but he tried hard to give the correct answers. His insides churned with anxiety. Little Meta noticed that she was not the center of attention and kept interrupting with silly and stupid questions.

"Daddy, what is 'skinit'?"

"Daddy, can I milk the cow, please?"

"Why does Emil have such big feet?"

At last, supper was over and Emil stomped out of the house. Once outside, he picked up one rock after another and threw them as hard and far as he was

23

able. Rock throwing was a talent he had developed as he grew strength in his arms. He was able to hit a selected object from a good distance. In defiance, he selected a mockingbird singing away in a tree nearby. He was not aware that little Meta had followed him outside until the bird came tumbling out of the tree, dead.

"Emil! You are a bad boy! You killed a bird!" she cried in a loud voice as she ran to pick it up and then cradled it in both her hands and reached them out to her brother.

"You are bad, Emil. You are so bad! I don't like you anymore. Now you have to bury it."

"Bury it yourself. I don't have time. Little girls are lucky. They don't have to work as hard as men do."

With that, Emil picked up one more rock and threw it at no particular target. He stomped off in the direction of the barn. He stopped and turned back to Meta. "I'm going to put the horses in the barn. Don't follow me. Otherwise, little girl, you just might get stepped on."

As Emil walked away from his little sister, he felt most regretful for his actions and words. He wished he could take them back. How he wished he could change things and just go back to being as happy and carefree as this past spring. Then, all the trees and grass and wildflowers just seemed to come out of nowhere overnight, and bluebonnets covered the small south pasture. Momma had insisted Papa must not let sheep graze in it, because they ate the young flowering plants. As a result, yellow Engelmann daisies were everywhere, and Indian Paintbrush and—

Emil smiled remembering how he'd opened the gate then to let the four waiting horses into the pen. Each horse knew exactly which stall to enter. He opened the rough wooden door of the adjoining grain bin and measured out the exact amount of feed and gave each horse its ration of oats. *Shoot,* he had thought at the time. *Why am I being so silly and bullheaded, anyway?*

"I can run this farm," he had muttered out loud. "Go fight for your stupid ideals, Papa. I'll show you! I can be a man."

Now Papa was actually gone. *Where is yesterday's bravado?* Emil asked himself.

Emil finished milking and let the calf in to join its mother. Then he took the pail of milk and headed toward the house. *First things first, that's what Papa would say. It is time to make some decisions. It is high time I stop complaining and do something right!*

Chapter Six

A rope was tied around Boerner's middle. His captors, on horseback, then made him walk behind them for hours. Herr Boerner, in his usual manner, had not spoken to the two men.

His quietness, however, did not keep his mind from whirling and pondering his fate. *And Elizabeth? Did she escape before they set fire to the house?* He felt sure that she had. *She's a smart little girl. We planned her escape carefully should this very crisis come to pass. It was not unexpected.* Yes. He had to trust that Elizabeth was going to be all right without him.

Boerner knew they were going in a northward direction. They might be heading for Fredericksburg and Fort Martin Scott. But Boerner was puzzled. These were not true Confederate soldiers. They were not wearing proper uniforms. But, in these turbulent times, there were so many self-appointed vigilante groups and militia units in Texas, who could keep track?

At last, the abductors stopped for the night. They made him sit against a tree trunk and tied him to it.

The next morning, time passed slowly, and with each agonizing step Boerner began to feel more hopeless. They had gone about three miles when the two riders halted their horses. It was in an area where some of the Union supporters had at one time hidden out. There were large oak trees, thick scrub oak underbrush, cedar, and several boulders. The three of them would now be well hidden from view.

One of the men ordered Herr Boerner to sit on a boulder out in the hot sun. After he was seated, the captors took their places in the shade of an oak tree and each took long drinks of water from their canteens. One took a second drink and then spat the water out at Herr Boerner's feet. Boerner said not a word but glared at the men in distaste. They had to know that he was very thirsty—especially in this awful Texas heat.

"Now we will have a little talk, Herr Boerner," the larger, heavier of the two men said. As he spoke, he again poured a trickle of water out of his canteen into the dust at Boerner's feet.

Boerner observed that his tormentor was not armed. When he'd dismounted, he left his rifle in the scabbard attached to his saddle. Boerner wanted to swift-kick the man in his groin but decided he could not win in this situation, not yet.

"If you give us the information we want, we will give you water. You won't be harmed—unless you refuse to talk."

Herr Boerner wanted, yes, could have begged for a drink of water. But he was not about to respond. Instead, he continued to glare at his captors in silent contempt.

"So, who is your leader, Herr Boerner? All we want is a name—or names. You Union sympathizers . . ."

The smaller of the two men now came forward and spat chewing tobacco on the rock where Boerner was sitting. It splattered on Boerner's arm. Boerner shifted his glare toward him but kept silent. His jaw worked and bulged in angry determination.

"Herr Boerner. You must understand. We are from the legal unit of the militia of the Third Frontier District—from the company of the Frontier Regiment of Texas. If you refuse to cooperate, we have authority to kill you as a Union spy, an act of treason."

Herr Boerner kept his eyes steady in a hard stare at his captors. He did not reply but kept his head raised in defiance.

"You ought to save your own life, you know? If you will speak, you might even save your daughter from harm." The heavier man smiled and sneered and showed broken brown, nasty teeth. Boerner flinched at the mention of his daughter.

He shifted his position on the hot rock—not only because of the heat of it, but because he was in great need to relieve himself.

"Ah! We have struck a raw nerve with Herr Boerner."

"Perhaps you are ready to talk?"

"How many are in the group of Union sympathizers? We know you know this, Herr Boerner. We've had our eyes on you for a long time. You're not as clever as you think."

"You are a German goose to be so stubborn," the second man added.

"You cannot win. The Confederacy will."

"You traitors had forty days to leave this state. Why didn't you go? Union forces will never come into Texas. *Dummkopf!*"

It was now after twelve o'clock noon. The men kept questioning Boerner without ceasing. They didn't offer him food or water. His throat was parched. He had not eaten since yesterday's supper, and his stomach growled.

Boerner finally spoke between clenched teeth, his voice steady and clear. "I need to relieve myself."

"Well, go ahead. We are not stopping you."

"You must untie my hands."

The heavier of the two said in a sarcastic voice. "Untie his hands, Jake. He will be more willing to talk when he is *more comfortable!*"

His hands were released. Boerner turned his back to the captors and quickly unbuttoned his pants and went about his business. Meanwhile, his eyes took in the situation around him. He wondered if he might make a break for it and escape. Only one of the men was holding a rifle on him; the other's rifle was in the scabbard on the saddle.

"Come now, Herr Boerner, return to the rock."

Boerner did not turn around. He thought they might shoot him in the back. That did not seem likely. They wanted information from him—they needed him alive.

"Take your seat now, Boerner. Don't even think you might escape."

Tension mounted with every word. But Boerner did not move. Perhaps he could entice one of them to come and physically make him move. Boerner was thinking that he just might then be able to overpower that one and use him as a shield. Would his partner shoot anyway, kill them both?

Boerner's mind raced with anticipation and possibilities.

"I will give you one more opportunity before I kill you, Boerner."

The voice burned like a piercing red-hot iron. Boerner stood rigid and still, his jaws locked. His ears were attuned to any move they might make.

He heard the click of the rifle hammer. An awful silence hung in the air. In a nearby tree, a mockingbird sang his song and punctured the scene below with intermittent notes. Time seemed to stand still.

Come and make me, Boerner thought, his heart pounding. *Just come a little closer to me and we'll see what kind of courage you have.*

Chapter Seven

Emil returned to the house with the morning's pail of milk. Following a talk with his mother and Elizabeth, it was decided that he and Lizzy would visit the Boerner house and see to the farm animals and Lizzy's dog. They would take feed for both. Emil also carried a rifle. At least his father had not left them without a means of protection.

Emma Schellhase watched the two children walk away. She held little Meta's hand a bit tighter than necessary. "Come back as quickly as you can. Be oh so careful."

"We will, Momma," Emil called back. "Don't worry. We'll keep our eyes open."

Emil Schellhase sounded much braver than he felt. But he knew Elizabeth was depending on him. He also thought again about some of the concerns he'd mulled over last night when he couldn't sleep—questions about all the pointless actions taking place in the community. Tensions around the Hill Country were becoming more stupid every day, he thought. What made people do what they do?

"Elizabeth, I feel so bad that your house got burned and your papa captured. Why would anyone want to do that?"

"Papa always warned me that this might happen. He spent lots of time explaining why."

"Do you understand any of this, Elizabeth?"

"Yes, I do, Emil. I really do. Papa says that when he and Momma decided to come to America it was because of some very bad things that had been happening in Germany for generations."

"Well, yes, I know all about that. The way they wished to free themselves from being overtaxed—even by the church. There were famines and no chance to better your place in life. Now there's quarreling and fighting here, too. We are not free here, either."

"Sometimes when you have freedom, Emil, you begin to take it all for granted and think it's yours forever. That's what Papa says."

"Well, I don't think fighting among ourselves does any good. But we better be quiet now and not talk anymore. We should also try to walk very quietly and try to not make any noise. Which way do you think will be the best so we can take a look at your place without being seen? Just in case somebody's come back."

"Follow me, Emil. I know exactly which way to go."

Lizzy stepped out in front of Emil. Without looking back to see if he was following, she made not a sound as she placed each tiny foot on small rocks and bare earth, working her way toward her home, or what was left of it.

As they were walking and came closer to the Boerner homestead, the smell of burned timber became stronger and stronger. Elizabeth's eyes filled with tears, and she had to stop to gather her wits about her.

She whispered, "I'm frightened at what we will find."

"I understand. Maybe you should just wait here. Let me go first."

"No—no. I'll be all right. It just hurts so badly. Papa worked day and night to build a place for us. Oh, Emil, what about my papa?"

"I don't know, Lizzy. Why do our papas allow such things to happen?"

"Allow such things to happen!" Elizabeth's voice was much too loud. Emil put his finger to his lips.

"Shhh, Lizzy."

Elizabeth had stopped walking and turned to look at Emil, her blue eyes blazing in utter disbelief. "Our papas did not ask for this."

"We'll talk about that at another time." Emil whispered in a voice that seemed strange to his ears. "Let's keep going."

Elizabeth walked on, but her steps were not as light as before. She walked in a heavy, determined, stiff manner. Emil was sorry he had not been more understanding. He should've kept his thoughts to himself. *Girls can be so sensitive!*

They walked the rest of the way in silence, and because there was a tension between them, which caused a bit of inattention to their surroundings, they came upon Fritz Vater, which surprised all of them.

Vater whirled around at the sound of the breaking twig under Emil's big foot.

"Emil! Elizabeth! You scared me half to death."

"What are you doing here, Fritz?" Elizabeth whispered.

"I came looking for your father, Lizzy. Instead, I find this." Fritz gestured toward the burned-out homestead.

The three old friends compared their stories and the circumstances of what brought them here. Vater told them he'd been watching for some time to see some movement or anything that might indicate that someone was on the premises. He reassured Emil and Elizabeth that it seemed safe to go on to inspect the burned-out home and barn.

"I will continue on to see if I can pick up their trail. Be careful and be safe."

With that agreement between them, Vater bade them farewell. He returned to where he'd tied up his horse, mounted it, and soon did find tracks. He glanced in the direction of the Boerner farm and saw the two teenagers walking down toward the burned home. He shook his head in sadness for them.

Elizabeth and Emil approached the house and barn in slow, painful steps. It was terrible to see the damage. The small barn was totally gone. It was fortunate the Boerners' milk cow had been safe out in the small field east of the dwelling.

The house! They were amazed to see that part of it, which was built of native limestone, hand-hewn rock, was still standing. And, even more astonishing, the main framework of the roof was not burned. The shingles were burned and gone, though. It was a mere shell. It was still smoldering and too hot to go inside, but they could see that several cast-iron pots and buckets and kitchenware were blackened but still usable.

Elizabeth fought back tears as she gazed upon the scene. She wanted to cry out in loud wails of pain, but it was a common German trait to suffer in silence and keep a stiff upper lip.

Emil went to see about Lizzy's dog. He had been staked out in the cornfield to guard the crop from invading raccoons. As Emil approached, the dog was leaping and jumping, straining against his restraint. The collie whimpered—he was frightened but seemingly unhurt. Emil unlatched his collar and the dog began to bark wildly and ran frantic circles around Emil.

Emil began to trot toward the house. "Let's go find Lizzy! Find Lizzy!" The dog caught up with him and, at the first glimpse of his beloved Lizzy, raced toward the house.

"Boerner! Oh, Boerner!" Elizabeth fell to her knees

and the dog barked and licked her face. As Emil came nearer, Boerner ran back and forth between them as if he couldn't decide which one to welcome the most.

They squatted on the ground together to hug the dog. They gave him the food and water they'd brought.

"Let's take your milk cow back to our barn. I'll milk her there."

Then Emil turned back to look at the house. "And that?" he asked in frustration, truly not knowing where to begin or what else to do.

"There were some important papers hidden in a hollowed-out rock on the east side of the kitchen wall. Also, my mother's jewelry—my momma's golden wedding band. Let's see what happened to that."

"Show me the place, Liz."

The two hurried to the outside of the still- standing eastern wall. Liz pointed to a rock just about a foot over her head. Emil examined it closely. He took out his pocketknife and found that it was possible to scratch away some of the lime mortar from around the stone. Before long, he was able to pull out the stone, which had been hollowed out on its inner side.

He set it on the ground with the open cavern facing up. Inserted into that cavity was a heavy black box! Emil pulled out the box, still warm from the fire. He handed it to Liz.

Elizabeth could speak only in short, whispering gasps. Her tiny hands were shaking as she feverishly set it on the ground, opened the latch, and turned back the hinged lid.

"It's all here! Safe and sound!" The impact of what this meant hit her full force then, and tears flowed down her cheeks.

"Oh, Emil, in this box are the 1854 land grants that show ownership of the land on which we're standing. Evil men can burn our house, but they will not be able to take our land."

"Your father was a smart man to think of that. I admire—"

"You sound like he's no longer alive! They wouldn't kill him—they wouldn't do that. Emil? Emil?"

Elizabeth stepped over the black box there on the ground and she was at him—pelting him on his chest with both little fists. He tried to back away from her sudden angry, screaming release of emotion, but he was too stunned to do anything but stand there and take it from her.

She kept coming at him until at last she was exhausted and spent. She leaned against Emil. "I'm sorry. I'm so sorry. This is all too . . ."

"It's all right, Liz." Emil held her now by both shoulders. He felt his own eyes tear up. He quickly released her and looked away. "We better head for home, Lizzy. I'll carry the box, and you lead your milk cow, since she's used to you. We'll come back later with the wagon and see what else we can salvage."

Emil's words were soft and gentle. His heart ached in empathy for Lizzy. He wanted to put his arms around her and comfort her. He'd seen his father do that often for his mother. However, something kept him from touching her again.

Elizabeth nodded without speaking and slowly, ever so slowly, took one step after another to begin the long walk back to Emil's house. "Come on, Boerner. At least I still have you and Ilsa, our milk cow. And," she lifted her chin in defiance, "this land."

The two young people, the dog, and the cow began the journey back to Emil's house. Emil tried to dismiss the fact that her father probably *was* hanged by now. The possibility was too real to deny. How did things get so out of control? How could grown men do such horrible and harmful things to each other?

The walk back to the Schellhase home was made in absolute silence. Words were not available to soothe away the terrible hurt and sadness. Perhaps tomorrow would be better.

Chapter Eight

Meanwhile, Karl Vater was able to track Herr Boerner and his captors without too much trouble. When he lost them, travelling often over those rocky parts of typical Texas Hill Country, he circled the area to pick them up again. It soon became apparent they were heading in a northerly direction—probably to Fredericksburg and Fort Martin Scott—assuming the captors were indeed Confederate soldiers.

But why kidnap Herr Boerner and burn his farm? Until now, the Confederacy had not made a practice of burning out farmers in this area of Texas.

Well, I cannot change that now. I have my mission, Karl thought. *I must hurry and try to get ahead of them somehow. Perhaps I could spy on them and identify the captors.*

Judging by the sun, it was close to noontime. Vater began to trot his horse a bit to gain ground. He was certain that he would be able to move faster than they would. He was one person on horseback, while they were, judging by the tracks, obviously still leading

Herr Boerner on foot behind their horses. *If I could pass them by and double back . . .*

Vater came over a small rise in the land and spotted them below. He immediately pulled his horse into the shade of a nearby tree and tied it to a branch. He took his rifle out of its scabbard and continued on foot.

It was a strange scene below. Herr Boerner had his back turned to his captors. Were they going to execute him?

Vater was grateful for the thick underbrush, dark cedars, and scrubby woods that concealed his approach. It was obvious that he had not been spotted, or they would have reacted.

Vater worked himself closer. He was able finally to hear their voices. They were demanding that Boerner turn around to face them!

Boerner spotted Vater crawling along the ground. Boerner almost smiled. *Das ist sehr gut.*

"Herr Boerner, I don't want to shoot you in the back, but I will if you don't turn around. Now! You are wasting precious time."

Herr Boerner heard the click of the rifle hammer behind him. He was certain that he was about to be shot in the back. *So be it, then. I will not be a traitor to my friends.*

"Why don't you come make me?" Boerner's voice was loud and took the captors by surprise.

The next scene seemed to play out in slow motion.

One of the captors approached Boerner, and, in a flash, Boerner spun around and with his strong large hands pinned the man's arms to his sides. He held the man as his shield. At that same moment, Fritz Vater stood up and took aim at the other captor, who held his rifle pointed at Boerner. Vater fired.

The captor saw Vater and simultaneously fired at him.

Both men hit their targets. Vater was more accurate. His man fell in a heap. Vater, bleeding from his chest, kept coming toward Herr Boerner, who continued to hold his man in an iron grip. Boerner, quick-thinking and quick-moving, grabbed the rope that had once held him bound. It became now the binding to disarm his abductor.

Vater's voice was coming in short gasping clips; "My horse is tied back—there. Go. Elizabeth needs her fath—" Vater fell to the ground.

"Here. Let me help you," Herr Boerner kneeled beside the wounded Vater.

"No! We have fired guns. It isn't safe here—go—now—"

"But what about this other one?"

Vater managed to raise his rifle just enough to fire at the remaining captor. It was at close range. He did not miss. "Now go—get away from here."

Vater collapsed. Boerner saw that Vater's shirt was soaked now with a huge bloodstain. He was there on the ground, very still, no longer breathing.

Herr Boerner ran to the captors' horses. He took their two extra canteens of water, their rifles, and dried beef jerky from the saddle pouches. He very soon found Vater's horse and rode away from the gruesome scene as fast as he could.

Boerner, being no stranger to these parts, knew exactly where he would go to hide out. No one would find him there.

Chapter Nine

Emma Schellhase was sitting in her homemade rocking chair holding the sleeping Meta on her lap. She sat near the window so that she might watch for her returning children. She glanced down at the child asleep in her arms and marveled at her sweet face and the curly blond hair. So like her daddy. *Oh, Fritz, how could you leave us?* Emma Schellhase's eyes filled with tears.

Emma rocked in a slow, steady motion and rested her head against the back of the rocker. If she and Edna had known what lay in store for them in Texas, would they have come to America anyway?

Scenes of her former life passed through her mind. What a time they'd had, she and Edna. They'd grown up together like sisters. Where one went, the other went also. Emma smiled as she recalled the good times they'd had dating Fritz Schellhase and Franz Boerner. Fritz and Franz! How many times did she and Edna sing out those names and then fall in a heap, laughing. Loving them had been so easy, and marriages were soon announced. Everyone had been so happy.

When the young Fritz and Franz began to talk of coming to America, it all seemed a glorious adventure to leave her beloved Germany and come to Texas—the "land of milk and honey."

Her own enthusiasm was never in question. Edna, on the other hand, was more reluctant. She was constantly asking questions. "What if we marry our gentlemen and we don't like America or Texas, what then?"

She remembered, too, how concerned their mothers had been at their talk of going to America. With tears, their mothers begged the girls to wait and follow Fritz and Franz at a later time.

But they were young and in love. What could possibly go wrong? Texas was touted to be the land that held every possible promise of wealth and happiness.

Emma's heart warmed at the memory of their weddings back in Germany. She had, of course, been Edna's maid of honor and vice versa. They ignored all warnings of possible unhappy events. They were full of hope and dreams of a bright future.

All that changed when Edna died of cholera aboard ship. Emma's heart was stunned, and she took Edna's little daughter into arms, and now she was like her own child. *Life takes strange turns*, Emma mused.

Emma opened her eyes. She could see the children now, walking ever so slowly toward the Schellhase farm. The weight of the world seemed to be on their shoulders. Emma rose and carefully laid the sleeping Meta in her cypress bed. The child stirred a bit, stuck her thumb in her mouth, and returned to sleep. Knowing she would be asleep for a good while, Emma reached behind the door for her bonnet and very quietly tiptoed out through the heavy wooden door. She must go to meet the youngsters.

Emma walked toward the teenagers with long, bouncing steps. She must show them courage and a brave spirit. They must never know how her heart was fainting under the burden of so much responsibility. *Fritz, you must come home safe, or God help us all!*

Chapter Ten

Emil and Elizabeth saw his mother coming out to meet them. Elizabeth wanted to run to her for the safety and comfort of those arms, but the milk cow she was leading made that impossible.

"Your mother almost bounces when she walks," Elizabeth said. "I hope I'll be like her when I grow up."

"I would say you're already quite grown up."

"Do tell, Emil. I didn't think you ever noticed such things."

Emil felt his face grow warm. He was glad he was walking in front of her.

"Oh, I notice a lot of things." He spoke with a smile that she couldn't see.

They walked on in self-conscious silence.

"Well! Are you going to tell me what you notice?" Elizabeth asked, trying to hurry the lazy milk cow so she could catch up to Emil.

"Of course! Someday I'll tell you." Emil replied without turning to look at her.

"Someday when we get married?" Her voice had an unmistakable lilt.

Emil stopped then and turned to face her.

"Married! Elizabeth Boerner! We're both too young to even think about that!"

Elizabeth kept on walking, leading the cow. She caught up to Emil, gave him a mischievous smile, and passed him by. He stood there in utter astonishment.

Emil continued to walk toward his mother. *Keep your mind on your business, Emil Schellhase.*

Emil observed the position of the sun and estimated the time to be almost twelve o'clock. Mentally, he made plans: He had to milk the Boerners' cow enough to relieve her overfilled udder and then—what? Perhaps later in the afternoon they would hitch up the draft horses to the wagon, return to the Boerner place, and salvage what they could from the burned-out house.

Emil thoughts also turned to Karl Vater. Would he find Elizabeth's father? And what about his own father? Where were they, and would they soon return to their farms and families? So many questions with no answers.

Emil squared back his shoulders and let out a sigh. *One step at a time. First things first. A real man does not whine.* In his father's words: A man has to do what a man has to do.

Deep inside, Emil wondered if he had the courage to take up that challenge. Only time would tell. For now, he must make every effort.

Chapter Eleven

Franz Boerner had ridden hard for almost an hour. During that time, he had seen no other riders or anyone else in these woods. He estimated by the position of the sun—and by how his stomach growled with hunger—that it was well past noon.

He halted the horse in the shade of a large oak tree, reached into the saddlebag, and grabbed a piece of the venison jerky. He dismounted to rest the horse a while as he chewed the hard-textured meat. He contemplated his plan of action.

Should he go back home to see about Elizabeth? Would he put her in danger if she knew he was alive? If she was questioned by anyone, friend or foe, it would be best for her if she didn't know.

With that difficult decision made, he felt a sudden sense of urgency. He mounted quickly and urged his horse forward.

He soon came to an area near his home. *Must I carry out my decision not to go there?*

The conflict within taunted him. *I can see no harm*

in riding by my farm to take a quick, short, secret look.

Boerner reined his horse south toward his farm—always making sure that the cedar brakes and oak trees concealed him.

He came finally to that place on his farm where he'd begun to clear out trees and underbrush to prepare a new field. He could now see his house and barn—or what remained of them. Intense determination and backbreaking work had gone into building up this place! In a matter of a few hours it had gone up in smoke!

It overwhelmed Franz to look upon the devastation. His heart ached with sadness. Then rage set in.

I have already given up my dear, sweet Edna. Now this farm, the improvements have been taken from me.

Boerner spat to the ground in rage. *How dare they go this far? I do not deserve this. I worked for this piece of Texas . . .*

Boerner remembered his land grants and all those things that were his most precious possessions. The black box! Did it survive the fire?

Without stopping to think that he was putting his safety in jeopardy, Franz urged his horse on toward the burned-out home. He rode there quickly and came around to that all-important rock wall, still standing. He saw in an instant that the hollowed-out stone had been removed and the black box was missing from inside! He cursed! Then his eyes spied—there on the ground around the wall—footprints in the black ashes and soot! One set of tiny prints and one set very large. A-ha! Of course! Franz smiled and nodded his head. *Elizabeth has learned her lessons well! They may ravage my farm, but they will not rob me of my land.*

At that moment, Boerner heard a spring wagon in the distance. He kicked his horse in its flanks and rode away in haste. He was not ready to be found. Not yet!

Chapter Twelve

It was a good thing Emil's mother was with the teenagers as they were driving the spring wagon toward Elizabeth's farm. She kept up an animated chatter with little Meta and in turn spoke with Emil and Elizabeth. Had it not been for her, there would have been total silence.

Emil and Elizabeth regarded each other with only brief, stolen glances. Whenever their eyes met, they quickly turned aside and looked away. It was not exactly an argument they'd had. Instead, a strange new uncertain feeling had come between them and destroyed their usual casual attitude toward each other. It bothered Emil that Elizabeth seemed always to be teasing him. Marriage indeed! Emil was relieved when they arrived at the Boerner farm.

Emma, Meta, and Elizabeth stayed in the wagon—at Emil's command! "I want to walk around the house and check things before you all get out."

Because Emil was a young man born to country ways and trained to observe such things, he noticed almost immediately that there were new hoof prints in the ashes and soot around the still-standing rock wall. He decided against pointing out the hoof prints to Elizabeth and his mother. There was no point in upsetting them with such news.

Who was on that horse? And what about that rock? We left it on the ground with the hollow side down. It has been turned on its side. New footprints, too. And what is this? A small piece of chewed dried venison—baking in the hot sun and crawling with ants! Emil kicked it away before anyone should see it. Strange.

They went to work but insisted Meta stay in the wagon—it was too dangerous to have her around the smoldering area. Emil, Elizabeth, and Mrs. Schellhase gathered up the black cast-iron pots and pans and loaded them into the wagon. They found also a blackened but not burned child's rocking chair. Elizabeth gently ran her hand over the hand-hewn wood, remembering how her father had built it for her one Christmas. She placed it in the wagon. Meta immediately sat in it and rocked.

The trio worked until it was time to return home to do the late-afternoon chores. Emil took his place on the spring-seat and drove the draft horses with expert hands. He felt quite grown-up—confident and wise beyond his years. Elizabeth took her place on the seat beside him and smiled at him. With admiring eyes, she said in a soft voice, "Thank you, Emil. I could not have stood coming here without your help."

Emil turned to look at her and smiled in return. He nodded but said nothing. He knew they were friends again. There was nothing more that needed saying.

Chapter Thirteen

A six-man military unit of Confederate soldiers made their way from Fredericksburg, riding to the small Hill Country settlement of Comfort. They were young men from local towns, Llano, Mason, and Kerrville. They, too, were recent immigrants from Germany and other foreign lands, and they had no wish to quarrel with anyone. They wore the issued uniforms because they had taken the required loyalty oath to the new Confederacy. While they did not adhere totally to that oath, they were good men who simply want to preserve the peace. They found themselves drafted into the Confederate Army trying to carry out the assigned mission: Investigate reports of rebellion against the Confederacy in the Comfort area.

Because they were all farm boys and well trained in the practice of country life, they observed buzzards circling off to the west of their route. They decided to check out the reason for such activity. Thus it was that the bodies of three dead men were discovered.

It was a gruesome find.

They chased away the buzzards doing what came natural to them—scouting food. Next, the bodies were searched for identification. They found a knife attached to the belt of the youngest one. The knife had a wooden handle carved with "K. Vater." They kept that for identification purposes. The other two bodies showed no form of identification. No uniforms—no hint at all.

The soldiers had some tools, but the hard ground made burial impossible. They quickly gathered rocks and covered the dead.

There was little talk between the soldiers. The youngest, having never seen a dead body, walked away and threw up. The others did not scoff or laugh, for this was not a proper time nor a laughing matter. This kind of incident was happening all too often in the Hill Country. They assumed this was yet another example of how awful and deep the disagreements were between people.

The Confederates tied the two riderless horses to a nearby tree. They would take them to Fredericksburg on their return trip to Fort Martin Scott. They would investigate the saddles for some identification. The knife would be turned over to the commandant of the Army post. They noted with interest there were no rifles to report.

Their job done, the soldiers rode on toward Comfort. They were silent. There was nothing to say. It is never easy to be confronted with one's own mortality. Life should never end with such violence.

Chapter Fourteen

In the early evening of that same day in the small hamlet of Comfort, the men assembled in the Brinkmann cellar took turns in the kitchen upstairs, where Frau Brinkmann cooked a huge pot of beans with smoked ham pieces.

Few words were exchanged between the men and Frau Brinkmann. The atmosphere was cordial enough, but, like the other wives, she was most distressed about the men's pending departure to join Union forces in Mexico. Like the other German women, she would support her husband and stand by in public in silence—no matter the pain.

Each man ate his ration quietly and quickly. Meanwhile, she packed venison jerky and hardtack in separate cloths for their trip. Each man would tote that in his own saddlebag. Each man also filled his canteen with water at the cistern. Then they left, one at a time, riding out of town without haste and by arrangement, going off in different directions. They would all assemble tonight at a secret designated place out in the hills west of Comfort.

After sundown that same day, the small military unit rode into Comfort. After the long, hot, and dry ride, they stopped at the Comfort Saloon to have a long drink of beer, eat some food, and listen for loose talk from the locals. They had done this assignment before, and the visits never disappointed them. Today seemed no different from any other.

Behind the long bar stood old Joe Pankratz, who was never talkative. At one of the several tables, four old men were enjoying a game of dominoes, a favorite of the German immigrants. They took notice but did not look up at the arrival of the Confederates.

The soldiers took their mugs of beer and seated themselves at two tables they'd shoved together. They sat back to observe and listen. Things seemed unusually quiet tonight.

Meanwhile, in the hills northwest of Comfort, almost one hundred men, fully equipped with bedrolls, rifles, mostly of antiquated German make, and six-shooters came riding in from several directions, from several Hill Country counties. This secret place was located almost in the middle of the vast Frederick Allerkamp land holdings.

The terrain, at first entrance to the land, was very ordinary: a gentle, flat surface. After about ten acres to the west, the land suddenly gave way to a steep drop into a seemingly typical Hill Country ravine. What was not so characteristic was the gigantic gray limestone rock that stood upright at the bottom of this drop. The rock stood next to a huge bluff from whence the single boulder must have tumbled eons ago. A cool, clear spring of water gushed out from under it. Surrounding the area were tall oaks and native walnut trees.

The men had met here in secret many times to receive messages and exchange information. Tonight's meeting marked the final phase of their plot to leave Texas via Mexico, then join the Union troops in New Orleans. It was a well-laid plan and a carefully kept secret. In a vote taken months ago, Fritz Schellhase, Emil's father, was elected the commander of the troops.

The following morning, August 1, 1862, they broke camp early. They were, at last, on their way to the Rio Grande under the guidance of Captain John Sansom, trusting in his experience as a Texas Ranger.

The die was cast.

Chapter Fifteen

Franz Boerner camped alone under the stars of Texas that night. He had earlier considered joining the men he knew would be leaving for Mexico, but he decided against it. Fritz Schellhase's family was depending on him to assist them in keeping their farm going. And his own daughter, Elizabeth, should not be without her father. He was comforted when he'd caught a secret glimpse of Fritz's family in the spring wagon yesterday as they approached the burned house. He was not surprised to see Elizabeth riding on the seat beside Emil.

Franz spread his saddle blanket on a bed of leaves. He reclined his weary body and rested his head on the saddle. His mind began to reel with questions and doubts about what he was doing: Shouldn't he let his daughter know he was alive? Must he stay hidden for while? Was he truly in danger? The incident of his kidnapping and subsequent death of his captors was not his fault.

There was also the haunting memory of Karl Vater.

He willingly gave up his own life to free me. I should not have left him there. I should have taken his body along, at least buried him! Should I go back there and do that?

The questions pounded away at him. *Why can I not go home a free man? I have done nothing wrong except help my friends and neighbors in their quest to preserve the Union of the United States of America.*

Franz's thoughts whirled around in circles. At last, beyond midnight, he fell into a fitful sleep. In troubled dreams, his deceased wife's beautiful young face smiled upon him, and she kissed him, gently brushing his lips. Over and over he called out her name. *Edna, Edna. I love you so. Lie down by me and keep me company. One day we will find our place in Texas . . . here so far across the sea.*

When Franz awoke, daylight was just beginning to drive away the night. His head was clear, and he knew somehow what he must do: he would stay hidden—at least for a while. The memories of Edna would keep him company—she would keep him safe.

He destroyed all evidence of his camp by taking a dry stick and scattering the leaves. Then, with his face set toward the west, Franz headed for that familiar rock on the Allerkamp land. There, he knew, would be berries and fresh water. He had enough dried jerky left to last at least a week; he also knew how to trap all forms of small wildlife and catch armadillo. *I will take one step at a time . . . one foot in front of the other.*

Chapter Sixteen

Emil's father has been gone for a little over a month, and it amazed Emil how easy it seemed to "take care of things." If Papa had to be gone, this was a good time of year to do so. The crops were harvested before his leaving and stored in either the barn or in haystacks; the animals seemed to be doing well; and Momma seemed to be taking the situation in stride.

Every morning, without fail, Emil milked both the Schellhase and the Boerner cows. The surplus milk was fed to the pigs and chickens. Emil also began to formulate in his mind another use for the extra milk. *I will keep that a secret until Christmas. Elizabeth will be so surprised and happy with me.*

In the meantime, Elizabeth had adapted well to living with the Schellhase family, and little Meta had become her constant, faithful shadow. Thankfully, Lizzy did not mind. One day she made little corn shuck dolls for Meta—a whole family of them. When she formed the mother and father dolls, her eyes filled with tears. Meta reacted quickly in sympathy and gently crawled onto Lizzy's lap. She laid her head on Lizzy's shoulder, and she reached her diminutive arms around the older girl's shoulders. "I love you, Lizzy. Don't cry."

Emil observed this affection between the girls, and his thoughts surprised and embarassed him. *I would like to comfort Lizzy like that.*

"That must not happen!" he murmured between clenched teeth when he was outside alone, thinking those thoughts. "I have work to do, and Lizzy will be just fine without me getting mixed up in all that girl stuff."

One morning, after the milking and the other chores were done, he went inside the house to get a drink from the cistern. His mother suggested they should go to town—to Comfort.

"Perhaps there will be some news of Papa and the men. It might even be possible that Papa will have sent us a letter."

Comfort was one of the first communities in Texas to establish a post office. Theodore Goldbeck was the postmaster, and Emma knew he could be trusted. Everyone was very proud of the new post office, even though it was in a small, narrow wooden store. Two years ago, Goldbeck's brother had helped to construct it.

Emil, very adept at harnessing up the horses, was ready to go in minutes. In no time at all, they were on their way. Elizabeth sat beside him on the spring seat, and his mother and the excited Meta sat on a blanket inside the wagon bed.

The road into Comfort was much used, but the rocky limestone surface, so typical of the Hill Country, was not given to smoothness. Little Meta laughed with joy with every bump and bounce. Nevertheless, they arrived in Comfort around eleven o'clock. Their first stop was the post office.

Emil climbed from the wagon, tied the horses to the hitching post, and slapped the dust off his pants. He entered the post office and said a cordial "Good morning" to Theo Goldbeck, who stood inside the postal window.

"Is there mail for Fritz Schellhase?" Emil felt very grown up. He had never done this before.

Herr Goldbeck's eyes locked with Emil's in a long, disbelieving stare. At last, he whispered, "Has no one been out to see you to tell you the news?"

"What is it, Herr Goldbeck? Tell what news?"

"Emil. You must come inside and sit. I'm afraid I have bad news."

Emil felt his legs turn to rubber, and he held on to the window frame with trembling hands. "Of course. Thank you."

Emil entered through the post office door, and Goldbeck indicated a chair for him. He sat quickly, but his eyes never left Goldbeck's face.

"What is it, Herr Goldbeck? What have you heard?"

"There was a spy in their midst. They were followed. They were ambushed at the western prong of the Nueces River. Many of our men were killed."

"My Papa? Was he . . . "

"I have no names, Emil. All I've heard, through whispered information, is that some escaped the bloodbath but we don't know who or where they are. If they are caught, they will be shot—or be hanged for treason."

"What can we do?" Emil felt sick to his stomach. "How can we find out who died and who escaped?"

"I wish I knew the answer to that. Emil, I think you should take your family home. Buy all the supplies today you might need for a while. If Fritz is still alive, he may hide out for a while and if he's able, he will get word to you. If I hear anything at all, I will ride out to your place to tell you."

"What do I tell my mother?

"I know it will be hard, but I would not tell her anything just yet. The secret will be easier to keep if only a few people know about the ambush."

"And Elizabeth Boerner? She is with us, too. Her father—"

"It's known to everyone what happened out there. It's also been rumored that three men were found dead between here and Fredericksburg. Karl Vater was identified as one of them. The other two were from the *Hängerbande*. The good news is Herr Boerner was not among the dead."

Emil stood up and rested his hands on Goldbeck's desk. "It's possible, then, that he escaped and is still alive?"

"I would not say that to his daughter—not yet."

Goldbeck stood also. He was not as tall as the young Emil was.

"Herr Goldbeck, I don't think I can keep all this a secret."

Goldbeck held up his hands to stop Emil from more talk. He felt a sudden impulse to hug this young man—to give him courage. Instead, he rested his hand on Emil's arm.

"You are strong, Emil. Your father said to me often what a fine son you are. Now you must prove that he was right. If your father is dead, we will find that out soon enough. If he escaped and is hiding out in the woods, you must keep the home fires burning. Or, if he is alive and has gone on to join the Union forces, you will do him proud by keeping your family and farm safe until he returns."

After Herr Goldbeck had spoken those challenging words to Emil, he reached out his hand and shook Emil's in a powerful exchange.

Emil felt a sudden surge of courage and determination. *My shoulders are broad and I am indeed strong.* He nodded his head. "I will do as you suggest, Herr Goldbeck. If you hear anything, we will be most grateful to you to send word. Have you any news from the war at all? Will it be over soon? I know Momma will ask."

Herr Goldbeck walked to the door with Emil. "No, son, I have no war news. We get the New Braunfels newspaper only on Saturday. Sometimes it is not so good to be living so far from the big city."

Herr Goldbeck walked out to the wagon with Emil and greeted the ladies cordially. He slipped little Meta a piece of hard candy and she screeched her delight. When she squealed, it frightened the horses, and Emil had his hands full to settle them down.

Next, Emil drove the horses and wagon to Ingenhuett's, the local general merchandise store. There were several horses tied up to the hitching posts. While Elizabeth and Meta climbed down from the wagon, Emil whispered to his mother that Herr Goldbeck had suggested they buy extra supplies and gradually get ready for a cold winter.

When she inquired if there had been any other news, Emil looked away. Her eyes seemed to bore into him.

"No, Momma. I would have told you right off. Come, let me help you down. We better hurry. Meta is loose in the store!"

Ingenhuett's was not the only store in Comfort in 1862, but it was certainly the best stocked. For the next hour, Meta was in heaven. Behind the glass showcases were candies and trinkets and a doll or two. She pressed her nose to the glass and pointed. Elizabeth kneeled beside her, and they talked excitedly about all those wonderful things.

While his mother shopped, Emil drifted to the back of the store. He engaged the older men, sitting around playing dominoes, in conversation. He asked them of any war news. They had none. They in turn asked about Elizabeth and said they'd heard about the burning of the Boerner place. They also asked about his father and how he was doing these days. Emil lied and said he'd gone to New Braunfels on business.

One of the men just sitting there was Herr Koerlin, from the furniture-making shop next door. Emil asked if he could see him privately. The two stepped out back. In only a few minutes, they returned and Emil shook hands with Herr Koerlin.

"*Danke schön* for your advice," Emil said. "I will try that."

Emil returned to his mother's side and helped her select sugar and flour and molasses to restock their supplies. He then whispered to his mother that he needed to buy some pumice.

Emma Schellhase gave her son a puzzled look. Emil pulled himself up to his tallest stance and whispered, "I just need it, Momma. It's a surprise for Elizabeth."

Emma selected a small bag of pumice and set it on the counter along with her purchases.

"Elizabeth? Is there anything you might need?"

Elizabeth was gazing at the ribbon counter with hunger in her eyes. "No, I think not—not today. Thank you."

"Buy us a ribbon, Momma. Please? Buy the blue that matches Lizzy's eyes."

Momma bought two blue ribbons, and Meta wandered off to the back of the store, where the men were playing. "Did you know I have a sister now?" she said to them.

"Oh, and what is your sister's name?"

"Lizzy. Lizzy Boerner."

"Is she Emil's sister, too?"

"No!"

"Why not?"

"'Cause they're going to get married." Meta drew out the words in an impish manner and then giggled.

The old men laughed in loud voices just as Emma came to get her daughter. "Come, Meta. We must not bother these men and their games!"

Emma fairly spat out the word *games,* as she had no respect for men who lolled around not working, especially when her own husband had gone off to fight in a war.

"And how is Herr Schellhase?" one of the men asked.

"He is just fine, thank you. Come, Meta. We must get back home before dark. *We* have work to do."

Emma Schellhase swept away from the men with Meta in tow. She walked so fast, poor Meta had to run to keep up with her.

"Momma? What did I do wrong?" Meta was not crying, but she knew her momma was very angry.

Emma Schellhase hurried out the front door of the store. She saw that Emil and Elizabeth were busy loading her purchases into the spring wagon. She hurried Meta along just as Emil was helping Elizabeth up to the seat.

"See, Momma? That's what I told the men in the store. Emil and Elizabeth are sweethearts—just like you and daddy!"

Meta was speaking in a rather loud voice. Elizabeth, perched on the wagon seat, giggled and smiled at Emil below. He quickly looked away as he waited to help his mother and sister onto the wagon.

Emil climbed aboard and sat stiff and straight on the wagon seat. His face burned red as he picked up the reins and flicked them over the horses' backs. Everyone but Emil was laughing out loud as they headed toward home. *Let them makes jokes. I have work to do! If they only knew—*

Chapter Seventeen

August 13, 1862

The familiar huge rock became his symbol of security as Franz Boerner continued to hide out on the Allerkamp land. Vater's horse, tied to a tree below the rock, was his only companion. The saddle hung from a nearby tree. Twice a day he led the horse down to the cool springwater. After he had allowed it to drink, he tethered it to another tree so it could graze on the native grasses.

Franz managed to say busy during the day. He explored the area around the campsite to find berries and signs of wildlife. He had not yet gone hungry, as he was a resourceful naturalist.

He also found some oats still hidden in a nearby hollow tree. He had brought the feed here himself to help support the Union sympathizers' horses. There was still a limited supply stored in a metal bucket with a lid. He rationed out a portion to Vater's horse every day.

It was almost nightfall. Franz walked upstream to where the clear springwater oozed from beneath the rock. He lay flat on his stomach and drank long from the cool spring. Then he stripped off his shirt and undershirt, washed his face and arms, and splashed cold water against his bare chest. Finally, he seated himself on a nearby flat rock and took off his shoes and socks. He eased his hot, tired feet into the cool water below. Franz closed his eyes and sighed in utter relief. He had not realized how extremely tired he was. He was feeling the lack of a proper diet, and sleeping out under the stars did not make for a good night's rest.

He still enjoyed occasional dreams of Edna. But he knew that he should not dwell too much on this desire to see her again—or he should go mad.

His stomach was growling in long, low rumbles. He inspected the stash of jerky he'd taken from the saddlebags. There were strips of the dried venison to last him for only a few more days. However, Franz reasoned, he knew he could trap rabbits—maybe even a small wild pig. And light a fire to roast them? Yes, he could make a small fire and then bury the meat in the ground with hot coals.

Franz Boerner sighed a tired sadness. He knew where he'd hidden peanuts, pecans, salt, and dried peaches—all survival food. It had been intended for his fellow compatriots while they were hidden out here on the Allerkamp land. *It never dawned on me that I would one day have to stay alive on those same staples.*

It was getting dark. Franz ate only enough to relieve his hunger pangs. Next he made a bed of old leaves, then a layer of green, and he spread the horse blanket over them. He rolled up his shirt for a pillow and laid the loaded rifle close beside him. It was not the most comfortable bed, but he was weary to the bone. In twenty minutes Franz Boerner was sound asleep.

He did not hear or see the riders come into his camp until it was too late.

Chapter Eighteen

The daily routine at the Schellhase farm continued without incident. September was approaching, and the subject of school dominated many conversations. Emil announced, in his newfound maturity, that he was not going to attend.

"I have work to do."

His mother said sharply, "Your education will not suffer because of that. Mrs. Altgelt is a good teacher, and we must support her or she may leave."

His mother was firm and unmovable. "I believe in the German tradition of a fine and broad education. And Elizabeth needs school, too. Emil, there is no discussion. You will accompany her there."

The subject became heated. It was three females against one male. Emil was frustrated beyond telling, and his temper flared often as the women seemed aligned to make him miserable.

"How am I supposed to work our farms when I'm sitting in school?"

Emma Schellhase placed both her hands on her

hips, and her eyes bored into Emil's until he had to look away.

"By the time the fields need plowing and the crops need planting, you will be back home again. I can take care of things while you're gone. Besides, Meta is growing up, and she will help me a lot."

"Yes, Emil. I'm a big girl now and I can help Momma a lot." Meta's hands were on her hips and her head tilted in an absolute mimic of her mother.

"I could stay with the Altgelts in Comfort for the school term," Elizabeth added. "Then Emil won't be bothered with me."

Elizabeth was neither smiling nor teasing. Her eyes never left Emil's face.

"I didn't say you were a bother." Emil ran his hand through his blond hair and scratched behind his ear. He suddenly remembered last year: Mrs. Algelt's son! He was always hanging around Elizabeth at school.

Elizabeth brightened. "I just thought of something else. Maybe if I went to say with the Altgelts, I could help take care of her children in return for my room and board."

"No, Lizzy!" Meta clasped her arms around Elizabeth's neck. "You have to stay here and take care of me."

"Children! Children! We will have no more argument. Emil, you're going to school, and Elizabeth, you will continue to live with us. Your mother would never forgive me if I let you go live with someone else. Now, everybody leave. We have work to do."

Emma Schellhase sounded much more confident than she was. She was deeply concerned about going through the winter and having to contend with all the problems that came with the season—especially with Herr Boerner absent. She dared not rely on their other neighbors. Many were in sympathy with the Union cause but made a wide berth around the Schellhase family because Fritz had been too outspoken.

Emma told herself, *I cannot be worried about what is ahead. Today was today and tomorrow will take care of itself. The children's education must not suffer because of the present situation. They will learn to read English, write, and do numbers. Mrs. Algelt promised she could teach if she could get students to come to her school in Comfort. So be it!*

Chapter Nineteen

August 14, 1862

The rising sun and the singing birds coming to water at the spring made for a calm, serene picture. Though Franz Boerner was not given to staying abed, this morning he did not want to open his eyes. He didn't want to face the new day. There were too many unanswered questions running around his brain. He rolled over. That's when he became aware of the presence of someone in camp.

Franz grabbed his rifle and jumped to his feet. He pointed the rifle at the two intruders. The sun was bright in his face, and the two were outlined against the brilliant light so that he could not see their features.

"Franz, Franz. Put down the gun! It's me, your old friend Fritz Schellhase and our Kerr County friend Gottlieb Stieler.

For the next hour, the friends sat and told about the events that had taken place while on the way to Mexico.

"Franz, we were attacked. At four in the morning,

while we were encamped at the Nueces River. And our muzzleloaders were a poor match against the breech-loading guns held by men covered in the cedar brakes. We ran out of ammunition by sunrise and realized how badly outnumbered we were.

"Finally it was every man for himself. Gottlieb and I made our escape together. We succeeded crossing an open space and we ran up the side of a hill. It has taken us five or six days to work our way back here. Prickly pear fruit and beargrass kept us from starving. It was bad, Franz. Very bad."

Gottlieb held his head in his hands. "Not many of us could have survived. We are now truly marked and wanted men."

"Franz," Fritz said, "the Confederates will be hunting us down as traitors and as enemies of the state of Texas."

Boerner reacted in curses and anger as he heard their story of horror and unbelievable violence. And after he finished telling them what had happened to him and his farm, and what had brought him to this place, the three knew that they were not safe, even in this secret hideaway. Time was running out. If a spy had infiltrated the Union alliance, nothing would keep him from knowing about this place.

The men kept a long, deliberating silence. Fritz Schellhase spoke first.

"If we stay together and play it smart, will it be possible for us to still get across the border into Mexico and possibly join the Union forces?"

Gottlieb Stieler cut off a piece of venison jerky and began to chew the hard, dried deer meat. "I think we have to try. We can't stay here. That would be a bad mistake . . . not only for us but for our families as well."

"I did not intend to leave my daughter before all this trouble," Boerner said. "But now, with the killing of the two men, Haengerbunder or not—even though I did not kill them—I, too, am a marked man. My life is impossible here alone. I can't go home. What do you think, Fritz? Can your family survive without me?"

"Emil is about as steady as any German I know, boy or man. I have seen him ride like a soldier. He runs like . . . well, in spite of his big feet, he can run like a deer. He is strong as an ox and smart, too. His mother will help him remember all the chores he does not like to do. Yes, I think we should go—together—to join the Union army. If we die in that attempt, we will at least have died honorably and not as traitors. I have nothing but contempt for that word!

"Do we dare let our families know? I think the time may have come to do that. But how?"

Only a dove cooing in the distance broke the silence in the camp.

Boerner answered, "Even though my house was torched and burned, there's a hollowed-out stone. We could leave a message in that and put the stone back in the wall. One day Emil and Elizabeth will discover it."

"You are a genius, Franz. Only you would think of such a thing!"

78

"I'll carve our names on one of these flat river rocks. I'll say, 'We are safe.'" Franz set to work immediately. By early evening he had completed their names on one side of the rock. He then turned it over and carved "Love and hope."

The three friends rested until the sky turned dark. They rode off together but separated as soon as they left the Allerkamp land. Franz rode to his homestead alone and placed the message rock inside the hollowed-out limestone and replaced it in the gaping hole in the wall.

The three riders, separated by only a few miles, rode until they were out of the Hill Country and well on their way to Mexico. They were cautious, did not ride in haste, and kept an ever-vigilant watch.

Franz arrived first at the planned location in Hidalgo and waited. In a matter of hours the trio was reunited. They rode through Mexico to Monterrey, some nine hundred miles, then to Veracruz, and from there they embarked for New Orleans. Here they enlisted in the United States Union Army, in the First Texas Cavalry Regiment.

Chapter Twenty

December 28, 1862

It was truly amazing to Emma Schellhase how well the farm was surviving without Fritz or Franz. In October, Herr Goldbeck had delivered to her the news that the men were probably all dead, having died in the Nueces battle at the hands of Confederates. Goldbeck rode out alone and gently told her the news, as sketchy as it was. Details were lacking, he said, but he wanted her to know.

Following the sad news, Emma had days when she could hardly put one foot in front of the other. The nights were worse. She was heartsick and angry about the injustice done to her husband and his compatriots. And by fellow Texans, at that! Many nights, sleep was impossible.

But survival won out at last. She came to realize that if she did not lift her head and face the future with a brave heart, this turn of events might ruin both her and her little family. She turned inward then to her inherent German stalwartness. Determination became her watchword. She became a woman of fierce conviction: nothing would stop her from being a good mother.

There was, however, one problem that vexed and perplexed her and tested that resolve. It was Emil.

Christmas Day, Emil was still doing fine. He'd just had a very proud moment. He'd worked so hard on Elizabeth's present. Mr. Koerlin had instructed him on how to restore Elizabeth's scorched rocking chair. He'd spent secret hours in the barn, rubbing it with pumice and cleaning it with the surplus milk. With his hard work, the black soot and smoke damage faded away. He was so proud as he presented it to Elizabeth as a Christmas present. Through happy tears, Elizabeth cried and cried as she thanked him over and over again. It reminded her of her father!

"Papa built it for me when I was just a little girl. It all seems so long ago. How hard you have worked, too! Oh, Emil! Thank you! Thank you!"

Emma watched the exchange between her children. *I've not seen Emil smile like that since his father's departure back in August.*

In a few short seconds, Emil's smile was destroyed by Elizabeth's next sentence.

"Now I want to tell all of you my news. Mrs. Altgelt has made me a proposition. In summer, when school is over for the year, she wants to take me back to Germany. She wants to sponsor me to a university there—she wants my education to continue at a higher level."

81

"Oh, Elizabeth! What an opportunity!" Emma's heart soared.

"Mrs. Altgelt's son will come, too. He is a very good student."

"Of course he is," Emil said in a sarcastic tone. "His mother is his teacher and he's her pet!"

"That's not fair, Emil," Elizabeth said sharply. "Robert works hard at his studies. You could learn from him!"

Meta was busy playing with her new cornshuck doll and did not pay too much attention until she became aware of the developing argument between Emil and Elizabeth.

"Emil, why are you mad at Lizzy?" she asked.

"We're not angry, Meta," Lizzy spoke gently. "My teacher just thinks I'm a good student and your brother is jealous! My teacher wants me to go back to Germany so I can learn to be a teacher, too. She says I shouldn't be content to live here in Texas and someday marry a farmer and—"

"So! That's it! A farmer's life is not good enough for you anymore?" Emil fairly spat out the words. "Well, la de da! I'm going outside for some fresh air. All this talk about how smart you are is making me sick!"

Emil bolted out the door, into the dark night. Emma felt his sadness tug at her. She understood Elizabeth's excitement about the coming summer. She also understood the blow just delivered to Emil's heart. She was not ignorant of how Emil was falling in love with this girl. Of course his world was shattered by her announcement of leaving.

"What should I do, Mother Schellhase? I didn't think he'd be so upset."

"It might be good if you have a long talk with him. You are the best friend he has. He just can't stand the thought of your leaving here."

Emma's eyes filled with sudden tears. "I understand how he feels. I rather feel that way myself. I will miss you, too. But I can't not accept this opportunity."

Meanwhile, Emil was inside the barn, crying bitter tears. *Elizabeth. Elizabeth. How can you do this to me?*

It was several days before Lizzy had an opportunity to speak with Emil alone. He was busy tossing hay with a pitchfork to the two milk cows when she walked up to gather eggs from the next haystack. They were alone together for the first time since Christmas Eve.

"Emil? I'm so sorry. I didn't expect you to get so upset with my news. Please talk to me."

Emil continued to toss hay to the cows.

"I wouldn't hurt you for anything, Emil. You're my best friend in all the world and—"

Emil threw the pitchfork into the hay and turned toward her.

"Then why didn't you tell me about all this before now? If we're such *good friends*, you might have said something—anything before you just blab it all out in front of my family. And I'll bet Robert Altgelt is on fire with joy that you're sharing a trip back to Germany?"

Elizabeth set her bucket of eggs in the shade. She seated herself on a large, flat rock nearby and motioned to Emil to sit beside her.

"Come. Please? We must resolve this, or I won't leave here this summer. Please, Emil, give me a chance to explain what Mrs. Altgelt has in mind."

Emil shook his head slowly and looked off into the distance—anywhere but her eyes. She was beginning to tear up. Seeing that broke his heart even more.

"How could you do this to me, Lizzy?" Emil said as he dropped down beside her and held his head in both his hands. He was close to tears himself. That was the last thing he wanted her to see.

"Emil? Do you remember the night when my house was burned and your horses were stolen and we were in your barn and I said something about the promise we'd made to each other when we were just little children?"

"Of course. I remember that night. I also remember our promise way back when we were little. Seems I recall it better than you do. If you had thought about it at all, you would not go back to Germany!" Emil was becoming angry again, and he wanted to run away from here—and her!

Elizabeth laid her small hand on Emil's arm. She turned to him. "Please hear what I have to say. Please listen to me. I'm begging, Emil. Please!"

Emil could not look at her. Instead, he picked up

one small rock after another and threw them at nothing in particular.

"What's the use? You've made up your mind to leave. It's just like my father when he left. He simply *told* me what he was going to do, and that was the end of it."

"You haven't let me finish! I'm also planning to *come back* to Texas after I graduate. I want to come back to keep my promise to you and to teach school in Comfort! Besides, while I'm in Germany, we can write to each other often. Time will fly by."

"I want to believe you, Lizzy. I do want to marry—!"

For the first time, Emil had spoken of marriage out loud. Immediately he jumped up, reached out his hands to her. He pulled her close to him and whispered, "You have always been my girlfriend. I can't stand the thought of anyone else . . ."

Elizabeth's head came only to Emil's chest, but she reached up and took his face between her tiny hands.

"We will marry each other, Emil. But not yet! We must see to it that we have a good life together. I really want to become a teacher and also your wife—someday. We are not ready for that. Not yet."

"How do I know that when you return to Germany and go to the university, you won't be smitten with some handsome university man and never return to me?"

"You must believe in me, Emil. Wait, I know! There's something we can do! Let's go back to my place and get that hollowed-out stone. Then let's write our promises to each other and then put them in the stone for safekeeping. Let's carry it to a secret place—somewhere here on your land. That way you can read it over and over whenever you please—whenever you get lonesome or worried."

Lizzy was dancing around, and Emil delighted in her excited chatter.

"We won't tell your mother or Meta about our plans. It will be our pledge to each other—from now until then."

"I'd like that. We'll go get the stone. Tomorrow will be the first day of the New Year, 1863. It's a perfect day to seal our promise inside the stone."

They agreed. When all the chores were done tomorrow morning, they would use the excuse that she wanted to go visit the house once more—somehow neither Meta nor his mother would come with them.

Emil gave her an embarrassed, shy peck near her ear. She smiled up at him. Then he pulled himself to his tallest stance and said, "We must hurry and finish our chores before dark!"

Emil felt a heavy load had been lifted from his shoulders.

Chapter Twenty-One

January 1, 1863

I guess plans are made to be broken, Emil thought as he drove the spring wagon to the Boerner farm alone. Elizabeth had come down with a terrible cold during the night, and Momma would not hear of her getting out of bed. When she told Emil the news, he decided he would go on to the Boerner farm anyway and bring back the heavy stone alone.

As he drove the horses toward the Boerners' place, Emil observed a Texas cold front threatening from the north. It would not be a pleasant task driving the horses back through a storm should it blow in before he got home. Emil flicked the reins over the horses' backs to hurry them along.

But he did not win the race. The north wind hit full force just as Emil swung the wagon around to the east side of the still-standing wall. Because it had not rained in some time, the wind and the wagon wheels whipped up a thick cloud of dust.

Emil brought the horses to a halt and braced himself against the blast. He wound the reins around the brake handle and jumped down to inspect the ground at closer range. The stone was gone!

It was only natural for Emil to look up at the wall expecting to see a gaping hole. It was there—back in its original place!

Emil quickly pulled the stone from the wall. He almost dropped it when a huge gust nearly blew him over.

He wouldn't have seen the flat rock fall out from inside the hollowed-out stone had it not fallen on his foot. He picked it up and saw letters carved into the stone!

WE ARE SAFE
FRITZ, FRANZ, AND GOTTLIEB

Emil turned the stone over and saw carved there:

LOVE AND HOPE

Emil's hands began to tremble. What did this mean? Who carved this message? When was it put there? Were both his father and Herr Boerner still alive?

The wind howled and alarmed the horses. Emil knew that he must get them home and into the barn. He lifted the hollowed-out stone into the bed of the spring wagon and laid the flat rock inside. What should he do? Should he tell his mother? Of course! Tell Elizabeth? *Of course! Hurry, Emil! Hurry!*

Emil gave the horses their head and they galloped

toward home. It was rough going. His hands hurt from the extreme cold and trying to control the horses. His father never allowed him to drive the horses at such speed. Now Emil knew why!

The spring wagon bucked and bounced. Emil didn't notice the flat rock fly over the side. When he got home, it was missing!

The bad weather lasted the rest of that week, and as it turned out, everyone got sick—his mother as well. Emil ran a temperature for two days, and the strange flat rock appeared in all his nightmares. He tried to tell his mother what he'd found, but she dismissed it as just so much fever talk.

Emil was better in a week. With the storm over, he walked back and forth over the wagon tracks he'd made. He said nothing about the rock to anyone. What could he say? Maybe it had been only a dream.

He searched for the rock every day. With each day's failure, he became silent and moody. His mother noticed his strange preoccupation, but she excused it. *Emil is taking Elizabeth's going away to Germany very hard. I must leave him alone to work out his sadness. It is better that way.*

Emil did whisper to Elizabeth that he'd brought the hollowed-out stone from her place and that it was hidden it in the barn. They agreed to write their promises that evening while Mother put Meta to bed.

"Momma always tells Meta stories. There will be ample time to write our pledges."

At eight o'clock, they met at the table. The coal oil lamp burned brightly, and Elizabeth was quick to complete her writing. She handed it to Emil. He read it and smiled.

"That's very nice. Thank you, Lizzy."

Emil struggled longer—with his handwriting. When at last he was finished, he showed it to her. She smiled and nodded without comment.

The next day, they folded their papers, one inside the other, enveloped them inside a clean cloth, and then laid them in the hollow of the stone. Emil placed a clean rock on top of them. Then they pushed the stone back into the corner of the barn and covered it with loose hay.

"I can leave happy now, Emil. You will be very proud of me when I return as Miss Boerner, the teacher."

Emil yearned to tell her about having found the rock with the carved message. What would she say? More importantly, what would she do? Would she change her mind and not go back to Germany?

No. No. Emil decided he must continue to search for the missing rock. *If I find it, maybe then I will tell her—and Momma, too.*

Chapter Twenty-Two

The Next Year, 1863

For Emil the year that followed was marked by three important dates. First was the day of Elizabeth's departure. Up to this point little Meta did not comprehend that Lizzy was actually going away. But when she saw Lizzy's trunk being loaded onto the spring wagon, she began to ask anxious questions. When she finally understood that Lizzy was *leaving*, all hell broke loose!

Now, Meta had developed a voice that could be heard from far away. When the eruption happened, Emma was down in the cellar to pack a few apples for Lizzy to take on her trip. She heard the awful sound of Meta's cry and thought that something terrible had happened upstairs. Emma ran up the steps. She found Lizzy kneeling on the floor beside Meta, trying to console the distraught little girl.

Emil, outside hitching up the horses to the spring wagon, had a near runaway! He struggled to calm the horses and held on with strong hands. The dog began to bark furiously. Emil staggered around in the dust and almost lost his footing. That's when and how he found the missing flat rock!

He made a quick decision. He pitched the rock into the toolbox under the spring seat. *There is no good reason to upset everyone now. Besides, what was its meaning anyway? It's been lost for almost five months now, and nothing has happened to make the rock significant. It was probably a sick joke by the vigilantes groups that still roamed the state.*

The family went together to deliver Elizabeth to the Altgelts' home. On the way, Meta sat as close to Lizzy as she could while bouncing around in the bed of the spring wagon. Her eyes never left Elizabeth's face, and she kept asking Lizzy, "Why are you leaving? Tell me again."

Elizabeth patiently answered each time, reassuring Meta, "I promise I will come back, and when I do I'll be your teacher!

Emil was grateful that Lizzy was not sitting beside him on the spring seat. He was used to the idea of her leaving and would face her departure without too much emotion—provided she did not cry. Nevertheless, his heart was heavy. *I'll almost be glad once she is gone. Then I can begin to count the days until she will return.*

So the deed was done. They arrived in Comfort that day late in May and left Elizabeth at the Altgelts'. The return trip was long and sad. Emma sat in the wagon bed, holding her precious Meta on her lap. Emil, perched on the spring seat, did not talk. One thought kept running through his mind: *Two years—two long years!*

When the trio returned to the Schellhase farm, Emil busied himself with the evening chores. That was good. *I must stay busy—busier than ever now. This summer I will repair the rock fences on our place and the Boerners', too. The barn also needs repairs. I wonder if I might try to rebuild the Boerners' home-stead. I should make a trip into Comfort and get some instructions from Mr. Koerlin. I could also fell more trees to complete the new field project that Herr Boerner had begun. Yes. That would be a good thing.*

Emil fell into his bed that night weary to the bone, and he fell asleep with only a little tossing and turning. Tomorrow would be the first day of the next two years.

Where is Elizabeth tonight? Is she thinking about me? I guess not—since she was so anxious to leave. I only hope that Robert Altgelt is not keeping her company. Damn Robert Altgelt, anyway!

The second big event of 1863 occurred sometime near summer's end. Emil had opportunity to confide in Mr. Goldbeck about finding the flat rock. Mr. Goldbeck became very excited. There was no doubt, he said, that it was good news and that his father and Herr Boerner had escaped the Massacre on the Nueces, as it was being called in some circles.

"It could be that they came back to hide in the familiar hills surrounding Comfort," he said. Then he added, "Since you never saw or heard any more from them, do you think, Emil, they have gone on to join the Union forces?"

There was no way to know for sure.

Also, Emil learned, according to Goldbeck, that the New Braunfels newspaper reported that the war was going in favor of the Confederates. The *Zeitung* stated that many Union soldiers had been taken prisoner.

"So, Emil, if your father and Herr Boerner did escape to fight in the war, only time will tell if they are indeed still alive. If I were in your shoes, Emil, I'd keep quiet about finding the rock. There's no point in giving your mother or Elizabeth false hope."

Goldbeck sighed. "But you are an intelligent young man. You decide for yourself what is best." He put his hand on Emil's shoulder and gave it a reassuring squeeze.

The third big event of the year came with Elizabeth's first letter! It was addressed to Emma and family. Emil was crushed that she had not sent him a special note. It was therefore a wonderful surprise to find another letter addressed to him tucked inside the envelope. After reading the family's letter out loud, he took his personal letter up to his loft. His heart was galloping and his hands shook as he read:

August 12, 1863
Dusseldorf, Germany
Dear Emil,

It seems a long, long time since I left Comfort. Our journey back to Germany was also long. I could have slept for an entire week after we finally arrived here. I became terribly seasick halfway here and am still in a weakened condition. Mrs. Altget is taking good care of me and I know I will be well soon.

I am enrolled in university and look forward to beginning my studies. The sooner I begin, the sooner I will finish.

I miss you all something fierce. Especially you, Emil. I hope you are not working too hard and are taking some time to play with Meta. I miss her so much.

This letter will be short as I have much to do before my first day of school on Monday. Please hold me in your thoughts and dreams. I plan to do likewise.

Yours, Liz

Emil read the letter three times and then carefully tucked it under his pillow. *Tonight I will compose a return letter, and tomorrow I'll ride into Comfort to mail it.* He also marked this day on the two-year calendar he'd made for himself.

His mother called out to him. Emil was pulled back to reality and work.

"*Ja*, Momma. I'm coming."

That night, Emil sat at the rough table and tried to compose his letter to Elizabeth. He had a terrible time trying to express himself on paper, and he worried that Lizzy might consider him to be "just a farmer" without the ability to write well. *I'll show her.* He began:

Comfort, Texas
September 12, 1863
Dear Elizabeth,

I have read your letter five times and I think I could recite it by hard. Thank you for writing it and I will now try to make my letters neet so you can reed it good.

I have been bisy doing a lot of work. Yeserday I rode over to your place. I'm thinking I mite try to rebild your house. Vhat do you think of that? Tell me, please, how you wood like it to look. I have asked Mr. koerlin to help me. He likes the idea.

Meta misses you a lot but not more than I do.

I try not to think about you to much but that is hard to do.

I hope you can make all yur studies real good and come back to Comfort and be a teacher. May be you can teach me to write beter! I am trying real hard.

Momma told me I won't have to go back to school this year because we have so much work to do. I'm glad because I heer the new teacher is not so nice as Mrs. Altgelt was. Is Robert Altgelt at school with you?

Please write to me again—a letter just for me again. I liked that very much.

Your Emil Schellhase

His mother wrote Elizabeth a letter, too, in German. Emil took the letters into town the next morning. At the post office, Mr. Goldbeck was anxious to read him the latest news. Again, according to the *New Braunfels Zeitung*, the Confederate army was "taking heavy casualities" and the Union soldiers were "suffering greatly without uniforms, shoes, and food."

Goldbeck laid the newspaper aside. "It might be better that your father and Herr Boerner never made it to fight for the Union cause."

"My father had a choice, Mr. Goldbeck. He made it, and that was that. I still think he should not have left his family. I am very bitter and angry about that. But I am working hard to make up for his absence.

I hope I never have to make such a choice when I grow up.

"Ah, but Emil, sometimes a man must take a stand. Your father did. He does not want you and Meta to grow up in a land that makes slaves out of people. You must think about that. If a government allows slavery—"

"But Herr Goldbeck. He did not own slaves. What business is it of his if other farmers do? That's the part I can't understand."

"It has to do with freedom, Emil. We came here because our German government and our church oppressed us. A slave is likewise oppressed. He cannot own land. He cannot make a living for himself. He does not own his own soul! He did not even choose to come to America. Families are torn apart and sold! Children are being sold to work for other masters. Could you approve of that, Emil?"

"I have never thought about it like that. I'm so busy these days—doing all the work alone on two farms—a slave to help might be very welcome!"

"What if *your* skin was black?" Goldbeck continued. "Would you be a slave to the white man?" He studied Emil's face with an intense, searching look.

Emil's felt his face turn red, and the scalp under his blond hair burned. He felt so uncomfortable he had to turn away. The angry thought occurred to him that his own father had virtually made a slave out of him—his own son—so he would be free to run off and fight in a dispute that was not of his making!

Emil opened his mouth to say that but thought better of it. Goldbeck had been very helpful to him these past months, and he realized how much he wanted and needed his help in the future.

Emil looked up at the position of the sun. "I must hurry on. I want to see Herr Koerlin before I leave town. He's going to help me rebuild the Boerners' home."

"Ah, young man, I have something else I must share with you. Be careful how you talk around town, Emil. Since the Nueces incident, feelings are running very high. It's hard to know who your friends are."

"But that's over and done with. Why are people still angry?"

"It is being rumored there was a spy who gave away the plan. Some have even suggested that *I* might be that spy."

"You? Herr Goldbeck a spy?" Emil started to laugh.

"I see a lot of people here in the post office—every day. I could have been the one; it would have been easy."

Goldbeck's thick, round glasses reflected the afternoon sun, and for a moment Emil had the strangest feeling. *Goldbeck is baiting me—to get a reaction to his words.*

Emil began to back away from the conversation. *I must get out of the post office.*

But Goldbeck followed Emil to the door.

"And you, too, Emil. Some people have whispered that *you* might have been so angry with your father that you became the spy! You did know everything that was going on."

At last, Emil was able to get away from Herr Goldbeck. There was now a knot burning in his stomach. The implication that he might have been the one to betray the Union supporters, leading to the massacre—sickening. Emil had planned to stop by Herr Koerlin's shop, but, at this moment, all he wanted was to leave town in a hurry. *What new worry has Herr Goldbeck inflicted on me?*

Emil regretted having spent so much time in Comfort. He gave the horse his head to hurry back to the farm. His mother would be very worried by now.

He was at full gallop when he saw two men step into his path. Emil's horse tried to stop, and it reared up in reaction to the sudden intrusion. One of the men caught the bridle of his horse.

Emil had no idea who these two were, but it was very evident they were not friendly. He gave no thought to his actions but kicked the horse in its flanks. It reared up again and took off running, knocking the intruders to the ground.

"You will pay for this, you traitor!" the second man shouted as Emil disappeared into the brush.

Emil didn't slow down until he got home. He put the overheated horse in the barn, stripped off the saddle, and ran to the house. It was terrible fear that made him run. *Momma and Meta have been home alone all afternoon! So vulnerable.*

Emil barged into the house and nearly frightened his poor mother to death.

"Emil! *Gott im Himmel!* What in thunder has gotten into you? You look like you've seen a ghost!"

Emil told his mother the entire story. He could find no good reason not to. As he saw it, there were terrible things going on in the settlement of Comfort, and, if they continued, no one was safe—especially the Schellhase family. They determined, then, that this was one more reason he must not attend school in Comfort this year.

In Emil's next letter to Elizabeth, he told her again about not going to school. He could not tell her about the unrest and awful, vicious rumors that were the reason for the decision.

In her responding letter she wrote:

Dusseldorf, Germany
December 1, 1863
My dear Emil,

    It upsets me greatly that you ae not attending classes this fall! I cannot understand why you would allow your education to suffer because of your farm work. Robert Altgelt is such a good student. He studies even harder than I do.

    Also, you ought to consider little Meta. If she sees the attitude you have about school, she will likely follow in your footsteps. Please reconsider

and let some of your work go undone. If re-
building my house is part of the problem, then I
would rather you not do that. Please, please!
Think about what you are doing!

Yours, Elizabeth

Emil read the letter and tucked it under his pillow along with his others. How could he explain without upsetting her even more? And that remark about Robert Altgelt! It hurt him to know that they were probably attending classes together while he was here trying to balance work between their two farms. That night he took pen in hand to try to explain:

Comfort, Texas
December 1, 1863
Dear Lizzy,

How I wish we could sit doun together and
hav a talk. There are so many thing I want to
diskuss with you but I'm afrad it will upset you
to much and then interfear with your studees.
You will just have to truss me in my dession. I
have very good reazons not to go into Comfort
more than nesessary. If it will help you to for-
give me I promise I will borow some books
from the school and try to studie here at home.
Also, I will practize my writing. Your handwrit-
ing is so neet and mine is so messy. Please let
me know soon what you think of this.

How I wish you were back in Comfort al-
raady. Write agan soon.

Your Emil Schellhase

The next morning Emil took the letters into Comfort to post them. Mr. Goldbeck welcomed him without mention of their last strange visit. Emil was less than cordial and after the business of posting the letter Emil was almost out the door before Goldbeck spoke.

"Emil? How is your mother getting along?"

"Fine. We are all having to work very hard."

"There is more news, Emil." Herr Goldbeck picked up the *New Braunfels Zeitung* and began to read.

"Abraham Lincoln has been reelected as President by a substantial margin. By this the North has told Lincoln to carry the war on to a victorious conclusion. After November, triumph for the Union will only be a matter or time."

"What has that to do with me?" Emil's voice indicated sarcasm.

"That means, if your father is still alive, once the war is over, he'll be coming—"

Emil exploded, his voice harsh.

"Herr Goldbeck. My father has been gone for two years and we have had no word from him. We, my mother and I, have accepted the fact that he is dead. Why bring up the possibility he may be alive? He left us to fend for ourselves and we've done just fine without him. Besides, it seems to me, we are fighting our own civil war right here in Comfort."

Emil felt much better and turned to leave. Goldbeck spoke again.

"Emil! Emil! I'm your *friend*. The rumors about us are bound to fade sooner or later. We must stick together. You're angry because I told you how some people are thinking. You *needed* to know. I am not a spy; nor are you. *We* know that."

Emil let out a long sigh and let his shoulders sag.

"Herr Goldbeck. I'm so tired of conflict. I want nothing more than peace among our people, and I need Elizabeth home again."

"I understand. But you must remain alert. There are dangers still around us. I heard about the trap laid for you the last time when you were leaving town. Let me close up the post and I'll ride out with you a ways."

"I can take care of myself."

"Yes. You are right, of course. But Emil, you must hear me and hear me well. Lose your anger, young man. We must deal with this matter with patience and kindness. Time will take care of the rest."

Goldbeck looked deep into Emil's eyes. *The boy is becoming a man.* He stuck out his hand, and the two shook hands in the old German tradition, acknowledging respect and friendship. Emil stood tall and walked out into the afternoon sun. He was most grateful for this conversation. It gave him hope.

Emil rode on to Ingenhuett's store—without incident. Goldbeck was right: patience and kindness are powerful weapons. Still, in the back of his mind came a nagging question: *How do I fit that into my father's absence?*

Emil entered the store. Several men were standing around the stove. When they saw Emil, all talking stopped. The only sound was the ticking of the large pendulum clock. Emil straightened himself to his tallest stance and nodded to them. It made him proud to observe that he was as tall or taller than they were. He walked past them, then nodded and spoke to Herr Ingenhuett in a loud, clear voice.

"I will need to borrow some books from the school this year. When the new teacher comes into town, could you find out for me if that's permissible?"

Herr Ingenhuett answered in a loud voice, intending it to be heard by the older men.

"I most certainly will, Emil. It would be nice if more people around here would take a deeper interest in learning. It would be time well spent."

"Herr Ingenhuett, I am planning to rebuild the burned-out Boerner house. I have spoken with Herr Altgelt at the sawmill. He has offered me a part-time job in exchange for shingles. If anyone should come into your store looking for work, I could use some help when the time comes to shingle the roof of the Boerner house."

"I'll see to it and let you know. Do you hear from Elizabeth often? She must be very happy that you are rebuilding her place. I just hope she's really coming back to Comfort after being in Germany and surrounded by a kinder, gentler people."

"I hear from her as often as possible and, to answer your other question, I have mentioned rebuilding to her but I don't think she believes me. And, yes, she is planning to come back. Sometimes I don't believe that!"

Emil and Herr Ingenhuett both laughed and went on about their business. Emil bought Meta a small bag of hard sugar candy and some new paper for letters to Elizabeth. He also bought himself a new lead pencil. He was spending so much time and energy practicing his handwriting that a pencil did not last long!

The men, gathered there in the store, had gone back to their own idle chatter. They had lost interest in listening to Emil and Herr Ingenhuett.

All except one. He was a close neighbor to the Schellhase farm. He slipped out of the store, got on his horse, and rode out of town in an awful big hurry.

Chapter Twenty-Three

1864–1865

During the rest of 1864 and the beginning of the 1865, Emil was one of the busiest people in the entire Comfort community. His mother wondered how he could maintain such high-level energy until she remembered that 1865 was the year Elizabeth was expected home. She was going to graduate at the end of May, but she had not written when she planned to be home.

Emil did not worry. Well, not much! When his doubts soared out of control, he went to the barn, dug the stone out of the piled-up hay, took out Elizabeth's note, and read it over and over again. He imagined hearing her voice and he felt reassured. Then he rode to her house to look at the progress they had made and take inventory of what still needed to be done.

He was pleased with the progress. One day last year, after Emil's visit in Ingenhuett's store, a group began to show up to help Emil. The workers had been organized by one of the men who'd been in the store and overheard his request for help!

Emil and his mother were surprised and overwhelmed with gratitude. Emma and Meta cooked food and brought it to the hungry crew. Word soon spread to the ladies of the community, and they also began to bring food. The project soon became a community celebration. It was hard for Emil to imagine another good thing that could happen except Elizabeth coming home. She would be so surprised!

Emil wanted so much to write her about the rebuilding and how it was happening. Since she had never encouraged the possibility that he might rebuild her house, because she wanted him in school instead, Emil decided that she probably did not believe he was capable! Well, fine. She would see with her own eyes when—*if*—she came home.

Emil also worked hard to study and read all the books the new teachers were happy to loan him. Louis von Breitenbach was one of them. Then came a Mr. W. Mueller; next a Mr. Adolph Rosenthal. This year, 1865, the Comfort community was awaiting the return of Mrs. Emma Murek Altgelt, the beloved teacher who had taken Elizabeth to Germany and sponsored her education in the University.

When Emil wrote to Elizabeth these days, his letters were much neater and quite learned! In composing what he hoped would be his last letter to Germany, Emil wrote slowly and carefully:

Comfort, Texas
March 12, 1865
My dear Elizabeth,

My heart sings at the idea that you will be home soon. Meta is walking on clouds and Momma is smiling more than usual these days. I hope you are looking forward to being home as much as we want you back here.

I have been hard at work running both our places. In the evenings I study hard. Don't you think my handwriting and spelling are better as a result? I can thank Mr. Louis von Breitenbach for that. He is a hard taskmaster. (What do you think of that big word?) I have read many books and am anxious to match wits with you now.

You will be surprised how pretty the country-side looks. We've had a lot of rain, unusual for this time of year. I think even the land is ready to welcome you home. I am more excited than you can imagine. Do you still look the same? Will I recognize you? Guess how often I think of you in a day. Please hurry home!

Yours, Emil Schellhase

Emil rode into town to post his letter. Mr. Goldbeck was beside himself with joy at seeing Emil. He waved the *New Braunfels Zeitung* at Emil as he walked into the post office.

"President Lincoln's second-term inaugural speech is in here! You must read it, Emil. It is magnificent."

Emil took the paper and folded it. "I am happy for Mr. Lincoln. But I do not agree that war must be fought to settle issues. In the last paper you saved for me, I read that 600,000 men and boys have died in this conflict! One of them may have been my father. Elizabeth's father was probably murdered simply because he supported Abraham Lincoln's Union cause."

"We have no evidence of their deaths. Quite to the contrary. The message on the rock must have come from them. They may still be alive."

"At that time maybe they were. But if they did make it north to fight alongside the Union troops, they're probably dead by now—one of those 600,000."

"I repeat, Emil, don't give up hope. You should always be optimistic until proven wrong. And the newspaper says here: 'Confederate currency has depreciated so badly that it buys nothing.' With worthless money, the war is bound to be over soon!"

"Herr Goldbeck, my mother and I are working very hard. We find that being busy keeps us from worrying about the war. To us, the war is as far away as Elizabeth!"

"Oh, that reminds me!" Herr Goldbeck placed a letter in the postal window and smiled at Emil's blushing face.

Emil picked it up and turned it over in his hands. "Thank you, Herr Goldbeck! I'll be in to see you again soon."

Clutching the letter to his chest, Emil hurried out to the spring wagon. He crawled up to the seat, took out his pocketknife, and, as fast as possible, sliced opened the envelope.

Only a single sheet! That is not like Elizabeth! He read:

February 1, 1865
Dusseldorf, Germany

Dearest Emil,

   This letter will be short, as my time is running out. I have much to study before my final examinations to graduate from University. If I complete my courses with satisfactory grades, I will quickly let you know that we will be coming home. Until then, I remain,

                    Sincerely Yours,
                    Elizabeth Boerner

Emil tucked the letter inside his pants pocket, grabbed up the reins, and gave the horses a quick flick of them. The spring wagon moved away from the post office. One hurried stop at Ingenhuett's to fill his mother's order and he was off toward home.

He drove the horses a bit faster than his father would have approved of. But his mind was racing with all the things he still wanted to accomplish before Elizabeth arrived. He'd already planted new trees to replace the ones that had been burned. One fig tree had survived the fire and was green from the recent rains. Now he wanted to plant some flowers in the yard around her house. His mother had saved seeds from last year.

Emil's heart was beating so fast that he had to take a deep breath every now and then just to calm down. He smiled from ear to ear as he unhitched the horses from the spring wagon and turned them into the corral. He carried his mother's new sack of cornmeal under one arm and swung the other arm back and forth, back and forth as he whistled his favorite tune. It was thus he entered the house.

"My, you're in good humor. Let me guess. There was a letter from Elizabeth!"

"Yes, ma'am. And guess what? She's taking her examinations and then she's coming home—if she passes them."

"Oh, Emil. It's been so long! Meta will be beyond happy! But perhaps we should not tell her—not yet. She will drive us both—"

"Let's tell her, Momma. Maybe she will be good like she is before Santa Claus comes."

"You're right, of course." Momma called out the back door to the yard, where Meta was playing with six new kittens. "Meta! Come inside, please. We have some good news for you."

Meta put her favorite black kitten down by its brothers and sisters. She walked away backward as the tiny kittens all followed her. "Momma, can I bring the kittens inside, please?"

"You know the answer to that, Meta. If not, I will remind you. No, you may not bring the kittens inside.

We start that and we won't be able to step out of the door. They'll either trip us or drive us crazy with their meowing. Besides, they have work to do. They must catch mice in the barn or we shall give them away."

"Shooo! Shooo! You gots to do lots of work if you want to live here." Meta stomped her feet and flapped her skirt at the kittens. They all turned tail and ran away toward their mother and the barn.

"I'm coming, Momma. I saw Emil come home. Did he bring me some candy?"

As Meta came closer to the house, Emil met her outside and picked her up and swung her around and around.

"Guess what, little chicken! Elizabeth is coming home!"

Emil carried Meta piggyback as she squealed and shouted. Emil thought his eardrums would burst. What a voice she had!

"When is she coming? Tonight? Tomorrow? Next week? Well, tell me, Emil! Tell! Tell!"

Emil set Meta down on the steps. "Slow down! We don't know yet."

Fixing Emil with an intense stare, Meta jumped up, put both her hands on her hips, and clamped her lips tightly shut. "What do you mean, we don't know yet?"

"Just that. Elizabeth has to take her tests at school and then she will come home. In the meantime, we have lots of work to finish her house and yard. You'll help me, won't you?"

Meta turned on her heels and started out the yard gate.

Emma stepped in her way. "Where are you going?"

"Over to Lizzy's house. I didn't finish sweeping her yard yesterday."

"Silly goose! It would be dark by the time you got there. No, no. We'll make our plans tonight, and then tomorrow we'll all go there together."

Later that night, after everyone was in bed, Emil lay awake a long time on his cornshuck mattress. His thoughts were tumultuous: *How soon is she coming? She did not mention Robert Altgelt . . . or Mrs. Altgelt. That seems a bit strange. I don't like Altgelt. I don't like his looks, especially his red hair! I don't like his wimpy voice! I don't like how smart he is!*

Emil fell asleep. In a dream, Elizabeth and Robert were talking and making eyes at each other and laughing. Emil tried to get her away from Robert. Every time Emil reached for her, Robert stepped between them and sneered at Emil. Emil swung his fists at Robert's face. He connected. There was an awful squishing sound, and blood gushed from Robert's nose as he fell to the ground. Elizabeth rushed to his side and screamed at Emil. "Now look what you've done. You killed Robert!"

Emil awoke with a start and sat up in bed. His heart was beating much too fast and his throat was parched and dry. Tomorrow morning, he decided, he must dig out their letters of promise and put this awful mistrust behind him. Damn Robert Altgelt, anyway! Elizabeth could not come home soon enough.

Chapter Twenty-Four

April 1865

Emil drove the wagon into Comfort to see if Elizabeth had written another letter. She had not. Herr Goldbeck insisted that Emil take the *New Braunfels Zeitung* home and carefully read the second inaugural speech given by President Abraham Lincoln on March 4, 1865.

Emil took the paper home and threw it atop his trunk at the foot of his bed, along with some of the books he'd borrowed from Mr. von Breitenbach. That night, after a pleasant day working at Elizabeth's house, Emil brought the newspaper down to the table to read by the light of the coal oil lamp. He examined the length of the article on the Lincoln address and laid it aside. It was too long to attempt to read. He did scan the last paragraph and was astonished at the words:

With malice toward none; with charity for all; with firmness in the right, as God gives us to see the right, let us strive on to finish the work we are in; to bind up the nation's wounds; to care for him who shall have borne the battle, and for his widow; and his orphan—to do all which may achieve and cherish a just, and a lasting peace, among ourselves, and with all nations.

Emil read that last paragraph several times. He understood now why Herr Goldbeck had insisted he should read it. President Abraham Lincoln had spoken words of peace. *I could agree to that.* But "To bind up the nation's wounds" was another matter. *When I consider the "wound" my father inflicted on Momma and this family. No.* To Emil's mind, his father's leaving to fight in the Civil War was not a subject open to debate. Emil knew his mother suffered greatly. In spite of her determined appearance, on many mornings Emil noticed deep, dark circles under her eyes. They were put there by his father's absence. He asked his mother often how he might help her. She always gave him the same blunt answer: "As a beginning, you might try to forgive your father, Emil. I have. He was a brave man. I loved him dearly."

On those occasions, Emil longed to tell his mother about the stone that was resting beside the bigger stone and the two promise letters hidden away in the barn under the hay. One day the right moment for telling would come.

That opportunity came the next day. While he and his mother were chopping weeds in their cotton field, he decided to introduce the subject.

"Momma? Do you ever think that Papa might still be alive?"

His mother stopped and stared at Emil. She leaned on her hoe. Immediate tears filled her eyes.

"Strange you should ask me that! Sometimes—when I think about him—he seems so alive. I can't describe the feeling exactly, but it's almost as if he is trying to say something to me."

Emil saw his mother's agony. He had yet to find the courage to physically reach out to her and comfort her. All he was able to say was, "Maybe we will know something soon. Herr Goldbeck says the newspapers are full of stories that the war is ending soon."

"I hope so. That war should never have begun." His mother dried her eyes on her apron as she took a deep breath and lifted her head to the sun.

"Momma? If *you* feel that way, how can you ask *me* to forgive Papa for leaving us to fight in that war?"

"Emil, there are things you don't understand about your father. He is a man of high integrity. Do you know what that means?"

"I have come across that word in the history books that Mr. von Breitenbach has lent me. I have read that President George Washington and other presidents had *integrity*. I did not think that word should be used to describe men other than presidents!" Emil laughed, thinking he'd made a very learned point with this mother.

"You're wrong about that, Emil. Your father has integrity, and you should know that."

"And you should listen to yourself, Momma! You are talking about Papa as if he's still alive!"

"That's what I mean, Emil. I simply cannot speak about him—dead. I wish I understood why I do that." His mother began chopping at the weeds with angry vengeance.

"Momma. There's something I need to tell you." The words were out of Emil's mouth and surprised even him.

"And what is that?" Momma stopped to look at Emil. There was such urgency in his voice.

"I have something to show you. It's in the barn."

Emil had such excitement in his words that Emma could not bring herself to focus on her work. She gave Emil permission to run on ahead of her. Emma followed to pick up Meta under the nearby shade tree where she was stationed to play.

By the time Emma and Meta reached the yard of their house, Emil was waiting on the front porch with the stone. His mother sat on the steps and Emil laid the stone in her lap and told her the entire story.

"Did Elizabeth know about this?" Emma asked in a whisper.

"No. I didn't tell her for the same reason I did not tell you."

"I suppose there was no point then—as I suppose there is no point now." Emma's voice rose in tearful, angry words.

"Why *did* you show it to me now, Emil? Why, am I holding on to this stone as if it would bring him back!"

Emma was suddenly furious and hurled the stone into the yard. It landed on a soft place where she had dug up the soil to put in a flowerbed. Emil ran to pick it up, hoping it was not broken.

Emma screamed at him, "Don't touch it! Leave it there! I've planted flowers there. Maybe if they grow up around it, it will be a memorial to your papa—and to Elizabeth's father, too."

Emma pulled herself to standing, weary to the bone. "We must get the evening chores done. This nonsense is not helping us get on with our lives. Meta, let's go find some eggs. I hope our hens have worked harder than we have today!"

Emil was sorry he'd shown the stone to his mother. He fought to keep his anger under control. Her attitude and her reaction offended him. But he did not pick up the stone. How he wished he'd kept it a secret. He had always taken a kind of comfort in knowing the stone was there, hidden in the barn. It was perhaps the last thing his father had touched.

Emil, too, stood up. His momma was right. There was work that needed doing. He whispered to himself, "Grow up, Emil Schellhase! Grow up!"

Chapter Twenty-Four

Endings and Beginnings, 1865

There were many savage battles fought before General Grant of the Union Army finally did what four other Union generals in four years had been unable to do. He caught Robert E. Lee, general of the Confederates. General Lee sent a note to General Grant offering to surrender.

These two soldiers met each other in the quiet of Appomattox Court House on April 6, 1865, to lay down their swords. Lee worried that, like most other leaders of rebellions throughout history, he would be taunted, imprisoned, or even hanged. Some Northern newspapers were calling for just that.

But, guided by President Abraham Lincoln's vision of a charitable peace, Grant did none of this. Instead, after receiving a promise from Lee not to take up arms again, the Union commander set Lee and his men free. The hungry and defeated troops were given food and the most generous of terms.

Even though the Civil War came to an end, Texans were late in hearing the news. They were late, too, in hearing the news that President Abraham Lincoln had been assassinated by a single bullet at Ford's theatre on April 14, 1865.

Newspapers reported that following the assassination, chaos and rage again gripped the North. The situation was volatile; the new peace, frail as it was, threatened to come undone. Lee condemned Lincoln's assassination and celebrated the end of slavery. "I am rejoiced!" he said. Wise leadership on both sides saved the peace and, ultimately, the country. The North did not retaliate against the South or seek to impose harsh terms. The remaining Southern armies surrendered. Most newspapers published Lee's command to his soldiers:

> Go home now, and if you make as good citizens as you have soldiers, you will do well. I shall always be proud of you. In Lincoln's words, there must be "no persecutions." We must become countrymen again.

Emil carefully read all those editorials and all accounts in Herr Goldbeck's *New Braunfels Zeitung* and then hurried home to tell his mother the news. Meanwhile, the stone, while not exactly forgotten, was surrounded by beautiful blooming bluebonnets. Whenever Emil or his mother glanced at the flowerbed, they paused for a moment in silence. But the rock was never spoken of again.

And then one day other news took priority in Emil's life. Elizabeth's last letter was under Emil's pillow, where he read it at every opportunity.

May 29, 1865
Dusseldorf, Germany

My dearest Emil,

    I have passed all examinations! The professors at university all tried to persuade me to stay in Germany for more studies. I considered that for what might have been one minute! I told them thank you, but no thank you! Robert A. is staying on in Germany, as he has a girlfriend in University now. I am happy for him, as is his mother.

    So, Mrs. Altgelt and I will be boarding ship for America in one week. We hope to be back on Texas soil by mid-August. Mr. Altgelt is meeting us in Galveston and will bring us home to Comfort. I know he would be happy to bring you along to Galveston with him, but please do not do that. I remember how seasick I became on the ship coming over here, and I would prefer you not see me in such a green condition. Wait for me in Comfort. They will deliver me to your house as quickly as possible.

    Emil, I have been very busy these past few weeks, and I have not been homesick for the first time in two years. But now that I am thinking of you and home again . . . I fear I may die of it!

    You asked if you would recognize me. Will I recognize you? Have you grown even taller? We

*are both eighteen years old! I'm sure you must
have grown. I have, too ... in some very no-
ticeable places!*

*I must hurry on now and begin to pack my
trunk. I am bringing some things for Meta,
your mother, and, yes, you too! I am not bringing many clothes, as I am also bringing lots of
books for us to read.*

Sweet dreams until I see you!

From your
Miss Elizabeth Boerner, Teacher

Emil tucked her letter under his pillow for the
tenth time and closed his eyes. He tried to picture her
in his mind, but the memory was rather dim. He did
remember her eyes, though! Eighteen! Yes! They were
eighteen now ... old enough to marry as they had
promised each other they would.

*Married! We could live at her house. But what if
she does not like the house as it had been recon-
structed? Oh, my! How can I possibly wait two long
months? I wish Papa was here so I could talk with
him. He always seemed so sure of himself in everything he did. Even if I did not always agree with him,
he was an intelligent man. Stubborn! But intelligent
and wise in his own way.*

Emil fell asleep. His dream was not exactly a night-
mare. Yet it was disturbing. He saw his father coming
up the path toward the house! He was limping—walking with a stick! He had a beard, such a long beard that

Emil did not recognize him until he heard him speak. He sounded so tired. He hugged Emil for the first time in his life! He hugged and squeezed Emil so tightly he could hardly breathe! He was choking . . . he was suffocating . . . Papa! Papa!

Emil awoke in a cold sweat! He stayed in bed for some time even though the sun was already shining into his small loft window. Suddenly Emil really came to!

"Momma?" Emil called out and stooped to look down into the kitchen. His mother was not in the house. *Momma is out doing my chores! She will be very upset with me!*

Emil pulled on his trousers and climbed down the loft ladder two rungs at a time. He could not imagine having overslept. His mother never allowed that to happen!

Emil hurried out the door and saw his mother returning, carrying the milk pail. Filled!

"Well! You've decided to make your presence known on this farm?" Emma's voice did not reflect the anger Emil expected.

"Why didn't you call me, Momma?"

"I was eighteen once myself, young man." Emma smiled at Emil with a mischievous gleam in her eyes.

Emil had not seen or heard his mother so seemingly carefree and happy in years. He wanted to tell her about his awful dream but reconsidered. He would not upset her with "Papa talk" again.

Meta did that!

Meta was also still in her bed when Emil and Momma entered the house. She was awake, but she had not crawled out of her bed.

"Momma?" she called out. "Where is Papa?"

Emma almost dropped the bucket she had just emptied.

"Meta!" she said sharply. "What about your papa?"

"He came in a dream last night! I dreamed he came home!" Meta slid out of bed now that she had everyone's attention.

"He was hurt, Momma. Hurt bad! I didn't like that dream."

"Child, I'm sorry you had a bad dream. Maybe next time it will be a better one"

"Momma, I had—" Emil started to tell his mother that he, too, had had a dream, but she interrupted.

"Enough of this talk! We need to finish up our morning chores. Then, since Lizzy will be home soon, we ought to make a trip to her house to see if we are actually done with it."

And so the subject of Papa was closed and no more was said.

Inside, Emma wanted to scream! *I had a dream, too . . . that was how I happened to awaken so early this morning! No! No! These children will not hear this from me! Nothing good can come of it.*

Later, at Elizabeth's house, Emil showed his mother how he had built a trap door in the cypress floor as access to Elizabeth's safe. Emil had hollowed out another stone and then sculpted a second stone lid so fine that no one could have identified it as a safe. It would be fireproof, to keep her valuables safe.

"Elizabeth will be very proud of all your work. I wonder though how she will like living here alone. She—"

"She may not be living alone, Momma." Emil gazed off in the distance. He would not meet his mother's eyes.

"Why, Emil! Whatever are you suggesting?" Emma, too, refused to look directly at her son.

"Time will tell, Momma." Emil scooped up Meta and carried her to the spring wagon. He smiled, wondering if he would be able to carry Elizabeth like that.

The next two months were plagued with endless problems. The rains stopped, and the heat was most oppressive. The animals were restless. The corn was harvested more by raccoons than by the Schellhase family. The other crops were not as plentiful as usual, either. Emil wondered if he was responsible for that.

Then, one of the two remaining horses got sick and Emil had to rush into Comfort to see if help was available. By the time Emil returned home, the horse was back on his feet and frisking around. Emil was afraid it might have eaten some jimson weed.

The next day Emil searched the horse pasture and found the poisonous plant growing alongside the west fence. Fortunately, he had taken a grubbing hoe and was able to dig it up, then carry it home, where he would burn it.

The land was terribly dry, and Emil was concerned that the wind might carry some sparks and start a grass fire. They carried several buckets of water to control the burn, then watched it carefully. At the end of the burning, Emil poured water on the ashes to make sure there were no live coals.

That night, no one slept soundly. Meta whimpered most of the night, and Emma was afraid she was getting ill. Emil was also coughing too much. Emma reasoned he had inhaled too much smoke. *Fritz, how can we go on? Everything was going along so well. Why all these problems now? Why did you leave us to fend for ourselves? Perhaps I should sell this land and take my family back to Germany!*

The very next day, the rains came in torrents. Emil, caught in the barn between showers, reread the notes he and Elizabeth had written. He had been so busy with all the problems on the farm that he had not realized that the end of the month of August had come. There had been no word from Elizabeth! He decided then to take the spring wagon into Comfort as soon as the rains let up to check the post office. Perhaps she had been delayed.

When Emil told his mother of his plans, she listed several items he was to pick up at Ingenhuett's store. Emil decided he should also return Herr von Breitenbach's books, as they would be needed for the new school year.

So, Emil drove into town but found no news at the post office. Herr Goldbeck showed Emil a copy of the latest *New Braunfels Zeitung* stating that men who had fought in the war were slowly beginning to return to their homes. Most of them were wounded in one way or another.

"So, Emil, do not lose hope."

"Forgive me, Herr Goldbeck, but today I am more concerned about Elizabeth. She was to be home in August."

"You did not know! Herr Altgelt left last week to meet their ship in Indianola. He has not returned. So, don't worry so much, Emil. These things take time. It could be that the rains have delayed them."

"I suppose you are right, Herr Goldbeck. If my father was to return to us, how might he do that—come home, I mean?"

"It's difficult to say. I would guess it all depends on where he is coming from. There are railroads. There's also the stagecoach, or he could ride in on his own horse. There are many possibilities."

Emil started for the door, and Herr Goldbeck, as always, walked him to his wagon.

"Emil, take heart. Whatever will be, will be. You have grown a lot in the last few years. You have done well. Things have a way of working themselves out. It takes patience. That's the hard part, patience."

"Thank you, Herr Goldbeck. You have been a mighty big friend to my family and me. I shall never forget that."

Emil was seated in the wagon, and with reins in hand, he flicked them over the horses' backs and slowly pulled away from the post office. He heard the approach of another wagon behind him, and he turned in the seat to see. Emil froze.

"Papa? Papa!"

Both stopped their horses and wagons in the middle of the muddy, rutted street. They both safely tied the reins to the side and climbed off their wagons. They were oblivious to the deep mud oozing around and over their shoes as they embraced. Emil was a few inches taller than his father.

Papa's red hair and beard were long and unkempt, and his clothes and body smelled of old dust and sweat. But neither one cared. Emil wept, unashamed of his tears of joy.

"Papa! Papa! You're home! Let me look at you."

"Yes, son. I'm home to stay. The war is over."

Herr Goldbeck watched them from the front of the post office. He did not want to interrupt this reunion.

After a while, he approached father and son, walking toward them near enough to speak. "You two go on together. I'll bring your wagon home later, Fritz."

"*Danke schön, mein Freund.*"

Emil helped his father climb up to the spring wagon seat, and father and son rode on together. Emil was the driver. His father was most satisfied and pleased to see his son's skill in handling the horses. He could not take his eyes off his son. Watching him was easier than talking. Emil had grown so tall! He had matured into manhood. His father had not thought a few years would make such a difference.

As Emil drove the wagon, his thoughts ran in circles. *Papa seems so old and tired! I am happy he is back. I cannot hate him. He is my father! I love him!*

Chapter Twenty-Five

The Reunion

The closer Emil and his father neared home, the faster Emil let the horses run. He fully expected his father to say something about slowing them down, but Papa didn't seem to notice.

At last they drove into the yard of their barn. Emil was surprised that Meta was not running out to meet him. *Did you bring me some candy, Emil?* Today there was no Meta.

Emil unhitched the horses while Fritz headed to the house. Emil watched his father; he had a decided limp. It puzzled him that no one was out on the porch to greet Papa. Were they out in the pasture?

He quickly turned his attention to the matter of unhitching the horses. By the time he had completed the chore, he saw that his father had disappeared into the house. Soon he heard the sounds of jubilation and, of course, the ever-so-loud voice of Meta shouting, "Papa! Papa!"

Emil imagined they were all crying by now. He hurried to the house to join in the celebration. He entered from the front porch and immediately became aware of an unusual quiet. He heard the clock's *tick tock, tick tock, tick tock*. He decided they must all have stepped out the back door. Emil moved toward the back door.

"Don't leave me here alone, Emil."

Emil turned toward the voice in an instant. There she was. Tears were running down her beautiful face, her blue eyes begging him to come closer. He was frozen in time for only a second, and then he moved toward her and took her in his arms. He was not able to speak above a whisper, for he, too, was now sobbing with joy.

"Elizabeth. Elizabeth. You're home. Welcome back."

That afternoon, even though it was late, Emil took Elizabeth to see her house. She was overcome with surprise and delight. She was left speechless at the beauty of the restored home.

Emil asked, "Will you be afraid to live here alone?"

She returned his anxious look with the words, "A promise is a promise, Emil. Is our stone still in your barn?"

"No. I moved it back here. Let me show you."

The two young people walked into the house. Elizabeth could no longer control her tears of joy. Meanwhile, Emil kneeled on the floor and lifted the trap door to reveal the stone. He lifted the lid and brought out their promise letters.

Elizabeth kneeled down beside him as he unfolded the yellowed papers. They read them to each other. Emil read his first:

January 1, 1863
*   I promise to wat for your saff return from*
Germany. I will love you efen when you are in
Germany. I want to mary you when you git
back from Germany. (signed)
*   Emil Schellhase*

Emil laughed. "I have improved my writing since then, don't you think?" Emil now handed her paper to Elizabeth. She was at it again! Tears were streaming from her beautiful blue eyes!

"Now it's my turn." Elizabeth unfolded her letter and smiled at her own juvenile handwriting. She read:

Dear Emil Schellhase,
*   You are my dearest and best friend in all the*
world. It makes me unhappy when you are sad.
So, while I am gone to Germany, please read
this often. I hope it will make you smile when
you read it. Please ask me to marry you when I
come home again. I promise to say yes.
*   Yours forever,*
*   Elizabeth Boerner,*
*   January 1, 1863*

Elizabeth folded her letter and placed it back in the hollowed-out stone. Emil did the same. He replaced the lid and closed the trap door. She gave him her tiny hand and he helped her up. There was no hesitation in his voice.

"So, will you marry me, Elizabeth Boerner?"

"Yes. I am ready to marry you and spend the rest of my life with you, Emil. Let's go tell your parents. And Meta! We'd better put cotton in our ears for that one. She has developed a voice as big as Texas!"

That evening, late as it was, Emma cooked the finest meal she'd cooked in two years. Then the celebration was topped off with the formal announcement of the engagement.

Later the family assembled on the front porch. Fritz held Meta on his lap, and Emma snuggled close to him. Emil and Elizabeth sat close together and held hands. A long silence hung between them all—even Meta was quiet. At last, she was the first to speak. Her voice was soft and gentle.

"Papa? I missed you so much. Where have you been so long?"

"That's a long, long story, child. Someday, when I'm not so tired, I'll tell you about it. For now, I'll just say that I missed you, too—all of you. So tonight, let's just rest easy knowing that the worst of times is over. We have survived, and now we must look to the future.

"And now, young lady, you give your papa a big goodnight kiss. It's your bedtime!" Emma squeezed Fritz's arm before she took Meta's hand.

Meta kissed her papa and then clasped her arms around Elizabeth's neck.

"Now that you're home, will you sleep by me again, Lizzy?"

"I sure will! I'll be in with you soon, Miss Meta. I have many stories to tell."

Emma and Meta left the porch. They lit the coal oil lamp inside for their regular bedtime ritual.

"Mr. Schellhase? Can you give me any information about my papa? He just was taken from our farm and we have never seen or heard from him again. What do you think happened to him?"

"My dear. I hoped and prayed I would live to be able to tell you. Your father and I left here together—after the awful thing that happened at the Nueces River. Since it was not safe to return home, we both were able to join the Union Army after many days of travel. We stayed together until—until he died in my arms from a musket ball to his heart at Gettysburg. He took a shot that should have come to me. I tried to pull him down when the assault came. I tried, Elizabeth." Fritz's voice trailed off in a haunted whisper. "I tried, Elizabeth. I tried. He was my best friend!"

Fritz held his head between both of his roughened hands and wept at the memory of his friend's death.

"Oh, Father Schellhase." Elizabeth moved to Fritz's side and comforted him. There were tears streaming down her face. Her voice was filled with emotion and tenderness.

"My papa was like that. He was always the protector. I think that's why he never really got over my momma's death. He was not able to save her from the cholera on our journey to America. That terrible guilt haunted him."

"He loved your mother with all his heart. And he loved you that much, too, Elizabeth. His dying words to me were—if I lived to come home—to remind you of two things: His love for you and the place where your land grants—"

"Emil and I found them exactly where he said they were! Papa was very smart to have hidden them there—along with my mother's wedding ring." Elizabeth now moved back to Emil and leaned against him. "Her ring will fit my finger perfectly," she said as she beamed at him.

Fritz stood up in slow, stiff movements. He reached into his pocket. "Your father also asked me to give you this, Elizabeth."

Elizabeth took a plain golden wedding band from his hand. She spoke not a word but simply sat and stared at the object in her hand, shaking her head in disbelief. At last, through tears, she smiled at Emil. "I will give this to you when you put my mother's ring on my finger."

"It will always be very special. I will cherish it forever." Emil held her for a short while. After a few moments, she tweaked Emil's nose and left to join the ladies' bedtime preparations inside. Before she left them, she stopped to embrace Emil's father without hesitation. "Good night, Papa Schellhase."

Elizabeth placed both her hands on Fritz's hands. "There are no words to express what comfort I feel knowing you were with Papa at the end. You and he sacrificed so much. You were two brave men among many. Thank you. I hope we can all live on in freedom now. Good night, my two dearest, sweetest men." She kissed Emil tenderly and went inside.

Emil and his father were now alone. The full moon had risen, and the soft light of it was awesome. Katydids and fireflies flickered, and a bullfrog accented the sounds of late summer.

Fritz broke the silence between father and son. "Emil, I hope you can find it in your heart to try and understand why I had to leave."

"Herr Goldbeck explained many things to me, Papa. It took me a long time to get over being angry with you. I was just a child when you left—"

"I know. I lay awake many nights in that unspeakably awful prison camp. I thought about that—how young you were when I left."

"You were in prison, Papa?"

"For many weeks—in Andersonville, Georgia. Emil, we suffered. Many died in that Confederate camp. We ate the horrible food only because we wanted to live. My wounds were deep and bad—bad enough to—"

"To what, Papa?"

"For them to use the maggots—for medicine."

"Maggots! Papa? Such torture is inhuman!"

"No! No! It was the most humane treatment the Confederates had! They had no medicines—no antiseptics! If a man had a rotting wound, they applied maggots! Maggots are one of the few insects that will only eat dead flesh! No, Emil, it was the only treatment that kept many men alive."

"Papa, how could you survive all that?"

"Only by the grace of God, Emil. There were rumors that over 13,000 prisoners died in confinement."

"I'm sorry. I don't think I will ever understand war."

"Emil, what I did, I had to do. It's possible that you won't be able to understand why it was necessary I go—until someday when you are older and have children of your own. Maybe then we can speak again and you will forgive me."

"But, Papa, I *have* forgiven you, and I found myself in the doing."

"Then I'm a happy man, son. Let's go to bed. I am weary to the bone. Tomorrow is a new day. Besides, we have a wedding to plan! I came home just in time! There are a few things I expect Herr Goldbeck did not teach you. Only a father can do that. Goodnight, son."

"Goodnight, Papa. I'm so glad you're home." There was an awkward pause. "I love you, Papa."

"And I love you, Emil. I'm sorry I did not say that before now. And thank you, Emil. Momma says you did just fine managing the farm."

Father and son embraced briefly and then headed to the door. Emil rushed ahead to hold the door so his father could enter first.

Fritz looked up at his tall son's face. It was hard to tell which man's smile was the brightest.

Epilogue

The wedding picture of the *real Emil Schellhase and his bride Lena
Bonn*. This picture of Emil and his bride surfaced *after* this story was
written—even though the author had no knowledge that there ever
was a *real* Emil—much less with the sire name of *Schellhase!* This
picture is included here to give honor to his name and to the entire
Schellhase family, who have long held positions of respect and integrity in history.

Alora (Mae) Durden-Nelson retired in 1997 after twenty-seven years as the Comfort School District's children's librarian. During that period she wrote puppet and stage plays (twice a year, every year) for fifth and sixth grades and served as producer/director of her Elementary Library Children's Theater project. One play, *The Case of the Easter Villains*, was published in *Plays Inc. Magazine* in 1976. Other writing experiences include: freelance reporter, stringer, and Society Editor for the *Kerrville Daily Times*; and she compiled and wrote *With Eternal Glory*, a history of the Immanual Lutheran Church in Comfort. She presently serves on several boards as Public Relations writer for The Comfort Public Educational Foundation and the Bill Gorman Memorial Scholarship Group; Comfort Public Library Board for several years and elected president in 1995 until her retirement in 1997. Her first retirement challenge was to research and write a history to promote the 1,100-acre Robert's Ranch, given to the YMCA. It was this research that helped to inspire this book, *Son of Defiance*. The Rising Star Masonic Lodge No. 429 of Center Point, Texas, honored her in 1997 with The Community Builder Award. Her first book, *I Just Called Her Momma*, was published in 2003.

Gregory J. Krauter, author of the foreword for this book, has intensely immersed himself in the endeavor of learning as much as possible about the history of the Comfort community and area, as well as its early residents. He has been a member and often director of the Comfort Heritage Foundation for over two decades, including serving as president for a number of terms and chairing a number of special committees and projects to date. Additionally, he recently began his sixteenth year as a director of the Kendall County Historical Commission. His roots are deep in Texas history! He is the great-great-grandson of a number of prominent pioneer families that originally settled the Texas Hill Country. He is currently the fifth generation to operate Ingenhuett General Store in Comfort, Texas. The store has been in his family since 1867 and is the oldest one in continuous operation in Texas.